GREAT SHORT STORIES
by Contemporary
Native American Writers

DOVER THRIFT EDITIONS

Edited by
Bob Blaisdell

DOVER PUBLICATIONS, INC.
MINEOLA, NEW YORK

DOVER THRIFT EDITIONS

GENERAL EDITOR: SUSAN L. RATTINER
EDITOR OF THIS VOLUME: ALISON DAURIO

Bibliographical Note

Great Short Stories by Contemporary Native American Writers is a new compilation, first published by Dover Publications, Inc., in 2014. Bob Blaisdell has selected the stories, provided the introductory Note and the biographical information at the beginning of each story.

International Standard Book Number

ISBN-13: 978-0-486-49095-3
ISBN-10: 0-486-49095-5

Manufactured in the United States by LSC Communications
49095506   2018
www.doverpublications.com

Note

I'M NOT SURE how to generalize these stories, except to remark that there is a disarming humor in many of them, while almost never an unrelenting grimness. Several are dramatizations of education: a child or a grown-up learning the world, a culture, a task, or a family history. Beth Piatote's gorgeous story, "Beading Lesson," has it all:

> Maybe next time you come they will be having a powwow at the prison and you can meet my students over there and they can show you their beadwork. I think they always have a powwow around November, around Veterans Day. Your cousin Carlisle and his family come over from Montana last time, and the only thing is, you got to go real early because it takes a long time to get all your things through security. They have to check all your regalia and last time they almost wouldn't let Carlisle take his staff in because they said it was too dangerous or something.
>
> What's that? Oh, that's all right. Just make it the same way on the other one and everyone will think you did it that way on purpose.

The first few stories in this anthology, which is arranged chronologically by date of first publication, may frustrate us at odd moments with their broad characterizations that verge on stereotypes, but they are each complicated by an artfulness and depiction of personally observed details of nineteenth-century Native American life and ways. In "The Soft-Hearted Sioux," for example, Zitkala-Sa tells of the dilemmas faced by a mission-educated young man:

> In the autumn of the tenth year I was sent back to my tribe to preach Christianity to them. With the white man's Bible in my

hand, and the white man's tender heart in my breast, I returned to my own people.

Wearing a foreigner's dress, I walked, a stranger, into my father's village.

Asking my way, for I had not forgotten my native tongue, an old man led me toward the tepee where my father lay. From my old companion I learned that my father had been sick many moons. As we drew near the tepee, I heard the chanting of a medicine-man within it. At once I wished to enter in and drive from my home the sorcerer of the plains, but the old warrior checked me. "Ho, wait outside until the medicine-man leaves your father," he said. While talking he scanned me from head to feet.

The best stories, like the best stories everywhere at all times, are intense and continually surprising, among them D'Arcy McNickle's "Train Time," about a white Indian agent who believes he is doing the best for the children he's sending away from the reservation to a boarding school. He clearly feels some uneasiness about his decision, a grave doubt that, as we read, dawns on us and leads us to hope that one day the "Major" himself may regret his act of coercion: "Whether the boy understood what was good for him or not, [the Major] meant to see to it that the right thing was done. And that was why, when he made up a quota of children to be sent to the school in Oregon, the name of Eneas Lamartine was included. The Major did not discuss it with him again, but he set the wheels in motion. The boy would go with the others. In time to come, he would understand. Possibly he would be grateful."

In Sherman Alexie's "War Dances," we feel as if the writer is discovering the story himself and extending conventional short-story boundaries as he composes it: we encounter an interview, a checklist, a poem, a critique of that poem, and continual jokes and revelations. Such unfoldings by Alexie in this particular narrative are comical, moving, and effective. Alexie has built his career reflecting on the everyday bewilderments of multicultural America and what it means, anyway, to identify oneself or others as Natives: "And then I saw him, another Native man, leaning against a wall near the gift shop. Well, maybe he was Asian; lots of those in Seattle. He was a small man, pale brown, with muscular arms and a soft belly. Maybe he was Mexican, which is really a kind of Indian, too, but not the kind that I needed. It was hard to tell sometimes what people were. Even brown people guessed at the identity of other brown people."

On the other hand, Duane Niatum's "Crow's Sun" is a steady moment by moment depiction of a young Naval serviceman's introduction to the warden of a Marine Corps brig. Thomas will have to travel in his mind through space and time to endure this initiation:

> Casually, as if just waking up, the Sergeant lets his eyes drift down to Thomas's shoes and the yellow line.
> "What's your name, boy?"
> "Young Thomas."
> The Sergeant's jaws flush; grow puffy. He lurches from his chair almost knocking it over.
> The muscles in Thomas's face tighten; his eyes thicken; narrow into tiny moons peering from behind a shield of fern. He sways slightly; stiffens his whole body, not sure what to expect from the man closing in. Grandson to Cedar Crow, Thomas feels his fingers change to claws, to a wing of thrashing spirit flying wildly inside his ear. (Be calm and steady now. This man's your enemy. Know his every move. Break him like a twig if he tries to harm you. Be the thunderbird in our song. I am Crow, your father.)

The stories take place from Canada to New Mexico, to the in-between borders mocked and dramatized in Thomas King's "Borders":

> "Citizenship?"
> "Blackfoot."
> "I know," said the woman, "and I'd be proud of being Blackfoot if I were Blackfoot. But you have to be American or Canadian."

There are also the borders and intersections of cultures, as Pauline Johnson describes it through the heroine of "A Red Girl's Reasoning": "She belonged to neither and still to both types of the cultured Indian. The solemn, silent, almost heavy manner of the one so commingled with the gesticulating Frenchiness and vivacity of the other, that one unfamiliar with native Canadian life would find it difficult to determine her nationality." Leslie Marmon Silko, who made her debut on the literary scene at age twenty-one, once said her "search for identity as a half-breed is . . . at the core of her writing."[1]

---

1. *Carriers of the Dream Wheel: Contemporary Native American Poetry*. Edited by Duane Niatum. New York: Harper and Row. 1975. 222.

One of my hopes for this volume is that it inspires more stories by Native writers about that most American theme: discovery.

I could not have found many of these stories or authors without the loving, dedicated work of a number of editors of previous anthologies, among them:

Margot Astrov. *The Winged Serpent: American Indian Prose and Poetry*. Boston: Beacon Press. 1992.

Laura Coltelli. *Winged Words: American Indian Writers Speak*. Lincoln: University of Nebraska Press. 1990.

Rayna Green. *That's What She Said: Contemporary Poetry and Fiction by Native American Women*. Bloomington, Indiana: Indiana University Press. 1984.

Institute of American Indian Arts. *Both Sides: New Work from the Institute of American Indian Arts, 1993–1994*. Santa Fe: The Institute of American Indian Arts. 1994.

Karen Kilcup. *Native American Women's Writing: An Anthology, c. 1800–1924*. Oxford, United Kingdom: Blackwell Publishers. 2000.

Thomas King. *All My Relations: An Anthology of Contemporary Canadian Native Fiction*. McClelland & Stewart Limited. Toronto. 1990.

Craig Lesley. *Talking Leaves: Contemporary Native American Short Stories*. New York: Dell Publishing. 1991.

Duane Niatum. *Carriers of the Dream Wheel: Contemporary Native American Poetry*. New York: Harper & Row. 1975.

Simon J. Ortiz. *Earth Power Coming: Short Fiction in Native American Literature*. Tsaile, Arizona: Navajo Community College Press. 1983.

Bernd C. Peyer. *The Singing Spirit: Early Short Stories by North American Indians*. Tucson: University of Arizona Press. 1991.

Kenneth Rosen. *The Man to Send Rain Clouds: Contemporary Stories by American Indians*. New York: Penguin Books. 1992.

Hertha D. Sweet Wong, Lauren Stuart Muller, Jane Sequoya Magdalena. *Reckonings: Contemporary Short Fiction by Native American Women*. New York: Oxford University Press. 2008.

Contents

A RED GIRL'S REASONING (1893)

Pauline Johnson

Emily Pauline Johnson (1861–1913) was born on the Six Nations Reserve near Brantford, Ontario. Her father was a Mohawk chief; she was related on her mother's side to the American novelist William Dean Howells. After her father died she wrote fiction to help support her family and soon became famous on the stage in North America and England, performing readings from her work—outfitting herself as a "Mohawk princess" until intermission, and then for her second act, dressing in an evening gown. In 1886 she changed her name to that of her grandfather, Tekahionwake, though she continued to publish poetry and stories as Pauline Johnson.

"A Red Girl's Reasoning" dramatizes a cultural clash between a mixed-race young woman and her white husband: "The country was all backwoods, and the Post miles and miles from even the semblance of civilization, and the lonely young Englishman's heart had gone out to the girl who, apart from speaking a very few words of English, was utterly uncivilized and uncultured, but had withal that marvellously innate refinement so universally possessed by the higher tribes of North American Indians." While stagy, the story achieves some degree of pathos and delivers a strong comeuppance to Christian prejudices.

"BE PRETTY GOOD to her, Charlie, my boy, or she'll balk sure as shooting."

That was what old Jimmy Robinson said to his brand new son-in-law, while they waited for the bride to reappear.

"Oh! you bet, there's no danger of much else. I'll be good to her, help me Heaven," replied Charlie McDonald, brightly.

"Yes, of course you will," answered the old man, "but don't you forget, there's a good big bit of her mother in her, and," closing his left eye significantly, "you don't understand these Indians as I do."

"But I'm just as fond of them, Mr. Robinson," Charlie said assertively, "and I get on with them too, now, don't I?"

"Yes, pretty well for a town boy; but when you have lived forty years among these people, as I have done; when you have had your wife as long as I have had mine—for there's no getting over it, Christine's disposition is as native as her mother's, every bit—and perhaps when you've owned for eighteen years a daughter as dutiful, as loving, as fearless, and, alas! as obstinate as that little piece you are stealing away from me today—I tell you, youngster, you'll know more than you know now. It is kindness for kindness, bullet for bullet, blood for blood. Remember, what you are, she will be," and the old Hudson Bay trader scrutinized Charlie McDonald's face like a detective.

It was a happy, fair face, good to look at, with a certain ripple of dimples somewhere about the mouth, and eyes that laughed out the very sunniness of their owner's soul. There was not a severe nor yet a weak line anywhere. He was a well-meaning young fellow, happily dispositioned, and a great favorite with the tribe at Robinson's Post, whither he had gone in the service of the Department of Agriculture, to assist the local agent through the tedium of a long census-taking.

As a boy he had had the Indian relic-hunting craze, as a youth he had studied Indian archaeology and folk-lore, as a man he consummated his predilections for Indianology by loving, winning, and marrying the quiet little daughter of the English trader, who himself had married a native woman twenty years ago. The country was all backwoods, and the Post miles and miles from even the semblance of civilization, and the lonely young Englishman's heart had gone out to the girl who, apart from speaking a very few words of English, was utterly uncivilized and uncultured, but had withal that marvellously innate refinement so universally possessed by the higher tribes of North American Indians.

Like all her race, observant, intuitive, having a horror of ridicule, consequently quick at acquirement and teachable in mental and social habits, she had developed from absolute pagan indifference into a sweet, elderly Christian woman, whose broken English, quiet manner, and still handsome copper-colored face, were the joy of old Robinson's declining years.

He had given their daughter Christine all the advantages of his own learning—which, if truthfully told, was not universal; but the girl had a fair common education, and the native adaptability to progress.

She belonged to neither and still to both types of the cultured Indian. The solemn, silent, almost heavy manner of the one so commingled with the gesticulating Frenchiness and vivacity of the other, that one unfamiliar with native Canadian life would find it difficult to determine her nationality.

She looked very pretty to Charles McDonald's loving eyes, as she reappeared in the doorway, holding her mother's hand and saying some happy words of farewell. Personally she looked much the same as her sisters, all Canada through, who are the offspring of red and white parentage—olive-complexioned, gray-eyed, black-haired, with figure slight and delicate, and the wistful, unfathomable expression in her whole face that turns one so heart-sick as they glance at the young Indians of today—it is the forerun-ner too frequently of "the white man's disease," consumption—but McDonald was pathetically in love, and thought her the most beautiful woman he had ever seen in his life.

There had not been much of a wedding ceremony. The priest had cantered through the service in Latin, pronounced the bene-diction in English, and congratulated the "happy couple" in Indian, as a compliment to the assembled tribe in the little amateur structure that did service at the post as a sanctuary.

But the knot was tied as firmly and indissolubly as if all Charlie McDonald's swell city friends had crushed themselves up against the chancel to congratulate him, and in his heart he was deeply thankful to escape the flower-pelting, white gloves, rice-throwing, and ponderous stupidity of a breakfast, and indeed all the regulation gimcracks of the usual marriage cele-brations, and it was with a hand trembling with absolute happi-ness that he assisted his little Indian wife into the old muddy buckboard that, hitched to an underbred-looking pony, was to convey them over the first stages of their journey. Then came more adieus, some hand-clasping, old Jimmy Robinson looking very serious just at the last, Mrs. Jimmy, stout, stolid, betraying nothing of visible emotion, and then the pony, rough-shod and shaggy, trudged on, while mutual hand-waves were kept up until the old Hudson Bay Post dropped out of sight, and the buckboard with its lightsome load of hearts, deliriously happy, jogged on over the uneven trail.

★ ★ ★

She was "all the rage" that winter at the provincial capital. The men called her a "deuced fine little woman." The ladies said she was "just the sweetest wildflower." Whereas she was really but an ordinary, pale, dark girl who spoke slowly and with a strong accent, who danced fairly well, sang acceptably, and never stirred outside the door without her husband.

Charles was proud of her; he was proud that she had "taken" so well among his friends, proud that she bore herself so complacently in the drawing-rooms of the wives of pompous Government officials, but doubly proud of her almost abject devotion to him. If ever a human being was worshipped that being was Charlie McDonald; it could scarcely have been otherwise; for the almost godlike strength of his passion for that little wife of his would have mastered and melted a far more invincible citadel than an already affectionate woman's heart.

Favorites socially, McDonald and his wife went everywhere. In fashionable circles she was "new"—a potent charm to acquire popularity, and the little velvet-clad figure was always the center of interest among all the women in the room. She always dressed in velvet. No woman in Canada, has she but the faintest dash of native blood in her veins, but loves velvets and silks. As beef to the Englishman, wine to the Frenchman, fads to the Yankee, so are velvet and silk to the Indian girl, be she wild as prairie grass, be she on the borders of civilization, or, having stepped within its boundary, mounted the steps of culture even under its superficial heights. "Such a dolling little appil blossom," said the wife of a local M.P., who brushed up her etiquette and English once a year at Ottawa. "Does she always laugh so sweetly, and gobble you up with those great big gray eyes of hers, when you are togetheah at home, Mr. McDonald? If so, I should think youah pooah brothah would feel himself terribly *de trop*."

He laughed lightly. "Yes, Mrs. Stuart, there are not two of Christie; she is the same at home and abroad, and as for Joe, he doesn't mind us a bit; he's no end fond of her." "I'm very glad he is. I always fancied he did not care for her, d'you know."

If ever a blunt woman existed it was Mrs. Stuart. She really meant nothing, but her remark bothered Charlie. He was fond of his brother, and jealous for Christie's popularity. So that night when he and Joe were having a pipe he said: "I've never asked you yet what you thought of her, Joe." A brief pause, then Joe spoke. "I'm glad she loves you."

"Why?"

"Because that girl has but two possibilities regarding humanity—love or hate."

"Humph! Does she love or hate *you*?"

"Ask her."

"You talk bosh. If she hated you, you'd get out. If she loved you I'd *make* you get out."

Joe McDonald whistled a little, then laughed. "Now that we are on the subject, I might as well ask—honestly, old man, wouldn't you and Christie prefer keeping house alone to having me always around?"

"Nonsense, sheer nonsense. Why, thunder, man, Christie's no end fond of you, and as for me—you surely don't want assurances from me?" "No, but I often think a young couple—" "Young couple be blowed! After a while when they want you and your old surveying chains, and spindle-legged tripod telescope kickshaws, farther west, I venture to say the little woman will cry her eyes out—won't you, Christie?" This last in a higher tone, as through clouds of tobacco smoke he caught sight of his wife passing the doorway.

She entered. "Oh no, I would not cry; I never do cry, but I would be heart-sore to lose you, Joe, and apart from that"—a little wickedly—"you may come in handy for an exchange some day, as Charlie does always say when he hoards up duplicate relics."

"Are Charlie and I duplicates?"

"Well—not exactly"—her head a little to one side, and eyeing them both merrily, while she slipped softly on to the arm of her husband's chair—"but, in the event of Charlie's failing me"—everyone laughed then. The "some day" that she spoke of was nearer than they thought. It came about in this wise.

There was a dance at the Lieutenant-Governor's, and the world and his wife were there. The nobs were in great feather that night, particularly the women, who flaunted about in new gowns and much splendor. Christie McDonald had a new gown also, but wore it with the utmost unconcern, and if she heard any of the flattering remarks made about her she at least appeared to disregard them.

"I never dreamed you could wear blue so splendidly," said Captain Logan, as they sat out a dance together.

"Indeed she can, though," interposed Mrs. Stuart, halting in one of her gracious sweeps down the room with her husband's private secretary.

"Don't shout so, captain. I can hear every sentence you uttah—of course Mrs. McDonald can wear blue—she has a morning gown of cadet blue that she is a picture in."

"You are both very kind," said Christie. "I like blue; it is the color of all the Hudson's Bay posts, and the factor's residence is always decorated in blue."

"Is it really? How interesting—do tell us some more of your old home, Mrs. McDonald; you so seldom speak of your life at the post, and we fellows so often wish to hear of it all," said Logan eagerly.

"Why do you not ask me of it, then?"

"Well—er, I'm sure I don't know; I'm fully interested in the Ind—in your people—your mother's people, I mean, but it always seems so personal, I suppose; and—a—a—"

"Perhaps you are, like all other white people, afraid to mention my nationality to me."

The captain winced, and Mrs. Stuart laughed uneasily. Joe McDonald was not far off, and he was listening, and chuckling, and saying to himself, "That's you, Christie, lay 'em out; it won't hurt 'em to know how they appear once in a while."

"Well, Captain Logan," she was saying, "what is it you would like to hear—of my people, or my parents, or myself?"

"All, all, my dear," cried Mrs. Stuart clamorously. "I'll speak for him—tell us of yourself and your mother—your father is delightful, I am sure—but then he is only an ordinary Englishman, not half as interesting as a foreigner, or—or, perhaps I should say, a native."

Christie laughed. "Yes," she said, "my father often teases my mother now about how *very* native she was when he married her; then, how could she have been otherwise? She did not know a word of English, and there was not another English-speaking person besides my father and his two companions within sixty miles."

"Two companions, eh? one a Catholic priest and the other a wine merchant, I suppose, and with your father in the Hudson Bay, they were good representatives of the pioneers in the New World," remarked Logan, waggishly.

"Oh, no, they were all Hudson Bay men. There were no rum-sellers and no missionaries in that part of the country then."

Mrs. Stuart looked puzzled. "*No missionaries?*" she repeated with an odd intonation.

Christie's insight was quick. There was a peculiar expression of interrogation in the eyes of her listeners, and the girl's blood leapt angrily up into her temples as she said hurriedly, "I know what you mean; I know what you are thinking. You are wondering how my parents were married—"

"Well—er, my dear, it seems peculiar—if there was no priest, and no magistrate, why—a—" Mrs. Stuart paused awkwardly.

"The marriage was performed by Indian rites," said Christie.

"Oh, do tell me about it; is the ceremony very interesting and quaint—are your chieftains anything like Buddhist priests?" It was Logan who spoke.

"Why, no," said the girl in amazement at that gentleman's ignorance. "There is no ceremony at all, save a feast. The two people just agree to live only with and for each other, and the man takes his wife to his home, just as you do. There is no ritual to bind them; they need none; an Indian's word was his law in those days, you know."

Mrs. Stuart stepped backwards. "Ah!" was all she said. Logan removed his eye-glass and stared blankly at Christie. "And did McDonald marry you in this singular fashion?" he questioned.

"Oh, no, we were married by Father O'Leary. Why do you ask?"

"Because if he had, I'd have blown his brains out tomorrow."

Mrs. Stuart's partner, who had hitherto been silent, coughed and began to twirl his cuff stud nervously, but nobody took any notice of him. Christie had risen, slowly, ominously—risen, with the dignity and pride of an empress.

"Captain Logan," she said, "what do you dare to say to me? What do you dare to mean? Do you presume to think it would not have been lawful for Charlie to marry me according to my people's rites? Do you for one instant dare to question that my parents were not as legally—"

"Don't, dear, don't," interrupted Mrs. Stuart hurriedly; "it is bad enough now, goodness knows; don't make—" Then she broke off blindly. Christie's eyes glared at the mumbling woman, at her uneasy partner, at the horrified captain. Then they rested on the McDonald brothers, who stood within earshot, Joe's face scarlet, her husband's white as ashes, with something in his eyes she had never seen before. It was Joe who saved the situation. Stepping quickly across towards his sister-in-law, he offered her his arm, saying, "The next dance is ours, I think, Christie."

Then Logan pulled himself together, and attempted to carry Mrs. Stuart off for the waltz, but for once in her life that lady had lost her head. "It is shocking!" she said, "outrageously shocking! I wonder if they told Mr. McDonald before he married her!" Then looking hurriedly round, she too saw the young husband's face—and knew that they had not.

"Humph! deuced nice kettle of fish—and poor old Charlie has always thought so much of honorable birth."

Logan thought he spoke in an undertone, but "poor old Charlie" heard him. He followed his wife and brother across the room. "Joe," he said, "will you see that a trap is called?" Then to Christie, "Joe will see that you get home all right." He wheeled on his heel then and left the ball-room.

Joe *did* see.

He tucked a poor, shivering, pallid little woman into a cab, and wound her bare throat up in the scarlet velvet cloak that was hanging uselessly over her arm. She crouched down beside him, saying, "I am so cold, Joe; I am so cold," but she did not seem to know enough to wrap herself up. Joe felt all through this long drive that nothing this side of Heaven would be so good as to die, and he was glad when the poor little voice at his elbow said, "What is he so angry at, Joe?"

"I don't know exactly, dear," he said gently, "but I think it was what you said about this Indian marriage."

"But why should I not have said it? Is there anything wrong about it?" she asked pitifully.

"Nothing, that I can see—there was no other way; but Charlie is very angry, and you must be brave and forgiving with him, Christie, dear."

"But I did never see him like that before, did you?"

"Once."

"When?"

"Oh, at college, one day, a boy tore his prayerbook in half, and threw it into the grate, just to be mean, you know. Our mother had given it to him at his confirmation."

"And did he look so?"

"About, but it all blew over in a day—Charlie's tempers are short and brisk. Just don't take any notice of him; run off to bed, and he'll have forgotten it by the morning."

They reached home at last. Christie said good-night quietly, going directly to her room. Joe went to his room also, filled a pipe and smoked for an hour. Across the passage he could hear her slippered feet pacing up and down, up and down the length of her apartment. There was something panther-like in those restless footfalls, a meaning velvetyness that made him shiver, and again he wished he were dead—or elsewhere.

After a time the hall door opened, and someone came upstairs, along the passage, and to the little woman's room. As he entered, she turned and faced him.

"Christie," he said harshly, "do you know what you have done?"

"Yes," taking a step nearer him, her whole soul springing up into her eyes, "I have angered you, Charlie, and—"

"Angered me? You have disgraced me; and, moreover, you have disgraced yourself and both your parents."

"*Disgraced?*"

"Yes, *disgraced*; you have literally declared to the whole city that your father and mother were never married, and that you are the child of—what shall we call it—love? certainly not legality."

Across the hallway sat Joe McDonald, his blood freezing; but it leapt into every vein like fire at the awful anguish in the little voice that cried simply, "Oh! Charlie!"

"How could you do it, how could you do it, Christie, without shame either for yourself or for me, let alone your parents?"

The voice was like an angry demon's—not a trace was there in it of the yellow-haired, blue-eyed, laughing-lipped boy who had driven away so gaily to the dance five hours before.

"Shame? Why should I be ashamed of the rites of my people any more than you should be ashamed of the customs of yours—of a marriage more sacred and holy than half of your white man's mockeries."

It was the voice of another nature in the girl—the love and the pleading were dead in it.

"Do you mean to tell me, Charlie—you who have studied my race and their laws for years—do you mean to tell me that, because there was no priest and no magistrate, my mother was not married? Do you mean to say that all my forefathers, for hundreds of years back, have been illegally born? If so, you blacken my ancestry beyond—beyond—beyond all reason."

"No, Christie, I would not be so brutal as that; but your father and mother live in more civilized times. Father O'Leary has been at the post for nearly twenty years. Why was not your father straight enough to have the ceremony performed when he *did* get the chance?"

The girl turned upon him with the face of a fury. "Do you suppose," she almost hissed, "that my mother would be married according to your *white* rites after she had been five years a wife, and I had been born in the meantime? *No*, a thousand times I say, *no*. When the priest came with his notions of Christianizing, and talked to them of re-marriage by the Church, my mother arose and said, 'Never—never—I have never had but this one husband; he has had none but me for wife, and to have you re-marry us would be to say as much to the whole world as that we had never been married before. You go away; *I* do not ask that *your* people be re-married; talk not so to me. I *am* married, and you or the Church cannot do or undo it.'"

"Your father was a fool not to insist upon the law, and so was the priest."

"Law? *My* people have *no* priest, and my nation cringes not to law. Our priest is purity, and our law is honor. Priest? Was there a *priest* at the most holy marriage known to humanity—that stainless marriage whose offspring is the God you white men told my pagan mother of?"

"Christie—you are *worse* than blasphemous; such a profane remark shows how little you understand the sanctity of the Christian faith—"

"I know what I *do* understand; it is that you are hating me because I told some of the beautiful customs of my people to Mrs. Stuart and those men."

"Pooh! who cares for them? It is not them; the trouble is they won't keep their mouths shut. Logan's a cad and will toss the whole tale about at the club before tomorrow night; and as for the Stuart woman, I'd like to know how I'm going to take you to Ottawa for presentation and the opening, while she is blabbing the whole miserable scandal in every drawing-room, and I'll be pointed out as a romantic fool, and you—as worse; I *can't* understand why your father didn't tell me before we were married; I at least might have warned you to never mention it." Something of recklessness rang up through his voice, just as the panther-likeness crept up from her footsteps and couched herself in hers. She spoke in tones quiet, soft, deadly.

"Before we were married! Oh! Charlie, would it have—made—any—difference?"

"God knows," he said, throwing himself into a chair, his blonde hair rumpled and wet. It was the only boyish thing about him now.

She walked towards him, then halted in the center of the room. "Charlie McDonald," she said, and it was as if a stone had spoken, "look up." He raised his head, startled by her tone. There was a threat in her eyes that, had his rage been less courageous, his pride less bitterly wounded, would have cowed him.

"There was no such time as that before our marriage, for *we are not married now*. Stop," she said, outstretching her palms against him as he sprang to his feet, "I tell you we are not married. Why should I recognize the rites of your nation when you do not acknowledge the rites of mine? According to your own words, my parents should have gone through your church ceremony as well as through an Indian contract; according to *my* words, *we* should go through an Indian contract as well as through a church marriage. If their union is illegal, so is ours. If you think my father is living in dishonor with my mother, my people will think I am living in dishonor with you. How do I know when another nation will come and conquer you as you white men conquered us? And they will have another marriage rite to perform, and they will tell us another truth, that you are not my husband, that you are but disgracing and dishonoring me, that you are keeping me here, not as your wife, but as your—your—*squaw*."

The terrible word had never passed her lips before, and the blood stained her face to her very temples. She snatched off her wedding ring and tossed it across the room, saying scornfully, "That thing is as empty to me as the Indian rites to you."

He caught her by the wrists; his small white teeth were locked tightly, his blue eyes blazed into hers.

"Christine, do you dare to doubt my honor towards you? *you*, whom I should have died for; do you *dare* to think I have kept you here, not as my wife, but—"

"Oh, God! You are hurting me; you are breaking my arm," she gasped.

The door was flung open, and Joe McDonald's sinewy hands clinched like vices on his brother's shoulders.

"Charlie, you're mad, mad as the devil. Let go of her this minute."

The girl staggered backwards as the iron fingers loosed her wrists. "Oh! Joe," she cried, "I am not his wife, and he says I am born—nameless."

"Here," said Joe, shoving his brother towards the door. "Go downstairs till you can collect your senses. If ever a being acted like an infernal fool, you're the man."

The young husband looked from one to the other, dazed by his wife's insult, abandoned to a fit of ridiculously childish temper. Blind as he was with passion, he remembered long afterwards seeing them standing there, his brother's face darkened with a scowl of anger—his wife, clad in the mockery of her ball dress, her scarlet velvet cloak half covering her bare brown neck and arms, her eyes like flames of fire, her face like a piece of sculptured graystone.

Without a word he flung himself furiously from the room, and immediately afterwards they heard the heavy hall door bang behind him.

"Can I do anything for you, Christie?" asked her brother-in-law calmly.

"No, thank you—unless—I think I would like a drink of water, please."

He brought her up a goblet filled with wine; her hand did not even tremble as she took it. As for Joe, a demon arose in his soul as he noticed she kept her wrists covered.

"Do you think he will come back?" she said.

"Oh, yes, of course; he'll be all right in the morning. Now go to bed like a good little girl and—and, I say, Christie, you can call me if you want anything; I'll be right here, you know."

"Thank you, Joe; you are kind—and good."

He returned then to his apartment. His pipe was out, but he picked up a newspaper instead, threw himself into an armchair, and in a half-hour was in the land of dreams.

When Charlie came home in the morning, after a six-mile walk into the country and back again, his foolish anger was dead and buried. Logan's "Poor old Charlie" did not ring so distinctly in his ears. Mrs. Stuart's horrified expression had faded considerably from his recollection. He thought only of that surprisingly tall, dark girl, whose eyes looked like coals, whose voice pierced him like a flint-tipped arrow. Ah, well, they would never quarrel again like that, he told himself. She loved him so, and would forgive him after he had talked quietly to her, and told her what an ass he was. She was simple-minded and awfully ignorant to pitch those old Indian laws at him in her fury, but he could not blame her; oh, no, he could not for one moment blame her. He had been terribly severe and unreasonable, and the horrid McDonald temper had got the better of him; and he loved her so. Oh! he loved her so! She would surely feel that, and forgive him, and—He went straight to his wife's room. The blue velvet evening dress lay on the chair into which he had thrown himself when he doomed his life's happiness by those two words, "God knows." A bunch of dead daffodils and her slippers were on the floor, everything—but Christie.

He went to his brother's bedroom door.

"Joe," he called, rapping nervously thereon; "Joe, wake up; where's Christie, d'you know?"

"Good Lord, no," gasped that youth, springing out of his arm-chair and opening the door.

As he did so a note fell from off the handle. Charlie's face blanched to his very hair while Joe read aloud, his voice weakening at every word:—

DEAR OLD JOE,—I went into your room at daylight to get that picture of the Post on your bookshelves. I hope you do not mind, but I kissed your hair while you slept; it was so curly, and yellow, and soft, just like his. Good-bye, Joe.

CHRISTIE

And when Joe looked into his brother's face and saw the anguish settle in those laughing blue eyes, the despair that drove the dimples away from that almost girlish mouth; when he realized that this boy was but four-and-twenty years old, and that all his future was perhaps darkened and shadowed for ever, a great, deep sorrow arose in his heart, and he forgot all things, all but the agony that rang up through the voice of the fair, handsome lad as he staggered forward, crying, "Oh! Joe—what shall I do—what shall I do!"

It was months and months before he found her, but during all that time he had never known a hopeless moment; discouraged he often was, but despondent, never. The sunniness of his ever-boyish heart radiated with a warmth that would have flooded a much deeper gloom than that which settled within his eager young life. Suffer? ah! yes, he suffered, not with locked teeth and stony stoicism, but with the masterful self-command, the reserve, the conquered bitterness of the still-water sort of nature, that is supposed to run to such depths. He tried to be bright, and his sweet old boyish self. He would laugh sometimes in a pitiful, pathetic fashion. He took to petting dogs, looking into their large, solemn eyes with his wistful, questioning blue ones; he would kiss them, as women sometimes do, and call them "dear old fellow," in tones that had tears; and once in the course of his travels, while at a little way-station, he discovered a huge St. Bernard imprisoned by some mischance in an empty freight car; the animal was nearly dead from starvation, and it seemed to salve his own sick heart to rescue back the dog's life. Nobody claimed the big starving creature, the train hands knew nothing of its owner, and gladly handed it over to its deliverer. "Hudson," he called it, and afterwards when Joe McDonald would relate the story of his brother's life he invariably terminated it with, "And I really believe that big lumbering brute saved him." From what, he was never known to say.

But all things end, and he heard of her at last. She had never returned to the Post, as he at first thought she would, but had gone to the little town of B——, in Ontario, where she was making her living at embroidery and plain sewing.

The September sun had set redly when at last he reached the outskirts of the town, opened up the wicket gate, and walked up the weedy, unkept path leading to the cottage where she lodged.

Even through the twilight, he could see her there, leaning on the rail of the verandah—oddly enough she had about her shoulders the scarlet velvet cloak she wore when he had flung himself so madly from the room that night.

The moment the lad saw her his heart swelled with a sudden heat, burning moisture leapt into his eyes, and clogged his long, boyish lashes. He bounded up the steps—"Christie," he said, and the word scorched his lips like audible flame.

She turned to him, and for a second stood magnetized by his passionately wistful face; her peculiar grayish eyes seemed to drink the very life of his unquenchable love, though the tears that suddenly sprang into his seemed to absorb every pulse of his body through those hungry, pleading eyes of his that had, oh! so often been blinded by her kisses when once her whole world lay in their blue depths.

"You will come back to me, Christie, my wife? My wife, you will let me love you again?"

She gave a singular little gasp, and shook her head. "Don't, oh! don't," he cried piteously. "You will come to me, dear? it is all such a bitter mistake—I did not understand. Oh! Christie, I did not understand, and you'll forgive me, and love me again, won't you—won't you?"

"No," said the girl with quick, indrawn breath.

He dashed the back of his hand across his wet eyelids. His lips were growing numb, and he bungled over the monosyllable "Why?"

"I do not like you," she answered quietly.

"God! Oh! God, what is there left?"

She did not appear to hear the heart-break in his voice; she stood like one wrapped in somber thought; no blaze, no tear, nothing in her eyes; no hardness, no tenderness about her mouth. The wind was blowing her cloak aside, and the only visible human life in her whole body was once when he spoke the muscles of her brown arm seemed to contract.

"But, darling, you are mine—*mine*—we are husband and wife! Oh, heaven, you must love me, you *must* come to me again."

"You cannot *make* me come," said the icy voice, "neither church, nor law, nor even"—and the voice softened—"nor even love can make a slave of a red girl."

"Heaven forbid it," he faltered. "No, Christie, I will never claim you without your love. What reunion would that be? But oh, Christie, you are lying to me, you are lying to yourself, you are lying to heaven."

She did not move. If only he could touch her he felt as sure of her yielding as he felt sure there was a hereafter. The memory of times when he had but to lay his hand on her hair to call a most passionate response from her filled his heart with a torture that choked all words before they reached his lips; at the thought of those days he forgot she was unapproachable, forgot how forbidding were her eyes, how stony her lips. Flinging himself forward, his knee on the chair at her side, his face pressed hardly in the folds of the cloak on her shoulder, he clasped his arms about her with a boyish petulance, saying, "Christie, Christie, my little girl-wife, I love you, I love you, and you are killing me."

She quivered from head to foot as his fair, wavy hair brushed her neck, his despairing face sank lower until his cheek, hot as fire, rested on the cool, olive flesh of her arm. A warm moisture oozed up through her skin, and as he felt its glow he looked up. Her teeth, white and cold, were locked over her under lip, and her eyes were as gray stones.

Not murderers alone know the agony of a death sentence.

"Is it all useless? all useless, dear?" he said, with lips starving for hers.

"All useless," she repeated. "I have no love for you now. You forfeited me and my heart months ago, when you said *those two words.*"

His arms fell away from her wearily, he arose mechanically, he placed his little gray checked cap on the back of his yellow curls, the old-time laughter was dead in the blue eyes that now looked scared and haunted, the boyishness and the dimples crept away for ever from the lips that quivered like a child's; he turned from her, but she had looked once into his face as the Law Giver must have looked at the land of Canaan outspread at his feet. She watched him go down the long path and through the picket gate, she watched the big yellowish dog that had waited for him lumber up on to its feet—stretch—then follow him. She was conscious of but two things, the vengeful lie in her soul, and a little space on her arm that his wet lashes had brushed.

It was hours afterwards when he reached his room. He had said nothing, done nothing—what use were words or deed? Old Jimmy Robinson was right; she had "balked" sure enough.

What a bare, hotelish room it was! He tossed off his coat and sat for ten minutes looking blankly at the sputtering gas jet. Then his whole life, desolate as a desert, loomed up before him with appalling distinctness. Throwing himself on the floor beside the bed, with clasped hands and arms outstretched on the white counterpane, he sobbed. "Oh! God, dear God, I thought you loved me; I thought you'd let me have her again, but you must be tired of me, tired of loving me too. I've nothing left now, nothing! it doesn't seem that I even have you tonight."

He lifted his face then, for his dog, big and clumsy and yellow, was licking at his sleeve.

THE SOFT-HEARTED SIOUX (1901)

Zitkala-Sa

Also known as Gertrude Simmons Bonnin (1876–1938), Zitkala-Sa was born in South Dakota at the Yankton Sioux Reservation. After attending a Quaker missionary school and Earlham College, she taught at the Carlisle Indian Industrial School in Pennsylvania. She began writing, returned to the reservation, and married a Yankton Sioux, Raymond Bonnin. While involved in various national Indian organizations, she edited *American Indian Magazine*. "The Soft-Hearted Sioux" is narrated by a young Christianized man who returns to his Sioux reservation as a missionary: "My son [his father tells him], your soft heart has unfitted you for everything!"

I.

Beside the open fire I sat within our tepee. With my red blanket wrapped tightly about my crossed legs, I was thinking of the coming season, my sixteenth winter. On either side of the wigwam were my parents. My father was whistling a tune between his teeth while polishing with his bare hands a red stone pipe he had recently carved. Almost in front of me, beyond the center fire, my old grandmother sat near the entranceway.

She turned her face toward her right and addressed most of her words to my mother. Now and then she spoke to me, but never did she allow her eyes to rest upon her daughter's husband, my father. It was only upon rare occasions that my grandmother said anything to him. Thus his ears were open and ready to catch the smallest wish she might express. Sometimes when my grandmother had been saying things which pleased him, my father used to comment upon them. At other times, when he could not approve of what was spoken, he used to work or smoke silently.

On this night my old grandmother began her talk about me. Filling the bowl of her red stone pipe with dry willow bark, she looked across at me.

"My grandchild, you are tall and are no longer a little boy." Narrowing her old eyes, she asked, "My grandchild, when are you going to bring here a handsome young woman?" I stared into the fire rather than meet her gaze. Waiting for my answer, she stooped forward and through the long stem drew a flame into the red stone pipe.

I smiled while my eyes were still fixed upon the bright fire, but I said nothing in reply. Turning to my mother, she offered her the pipe. I glanced at my grandmother. The loose buckskin sleeve fell off at her elbow and showed a wrist covered with silver bracelets. Holding up the fingers of her left hand, she named off the desirable young women of our village.

"Which one, my grandchild, which one?" she questioned.

"Hoh!" I said, pulling at my blanket in confusion. "Not yet!" Here my mother passed the pipe over the fire to my father. Then she too began speaking of what I should do.

"My son, be always active. Do not dislike a long hunt. Learn to provide much buffalo meat and many buckskins before you bring home a wife." Presently my father gave the pipe to my grandmother, and he took his turn in the exhortations.

"Ho, my son, I have been counting in my heart the bravest warriors of our people. There is not one of them who won his title in his sixteenth winter. My son, it is a great thing for some brave of sixteen winters to do."

Not a word had I to give in answer. I knew well the fame of my warrior father. He had earned the right of speaking such words, though even he himself was a brave only at my age. Refusing to smoke my grandmother's pipe because my heart was too much stirred by their words, and sorely troubled with a fear lest I should disappoint them, I arose to go. Drawing my blanket over my shoulders, I said, as I stepped toward the entranceway: "I go to hobble my pony. It is now late in the night."

II.

Nine winters' snows had buried deep that night when my old grandmother, together with my father and mother, designed my future with the glow of a camp fire upon it.

Yet I did not grow up the warrior, huntsman, and husband I was to have been. At the mission school I learned it was wrong to kill. Nine winters I hunted for the soft heart of Christ, and prayed for the huntsmen who chased the buffalo on the plains.

In the autumn of the tenth year I was sent back to my tribe to preach Christianity to them. With the white man's Bible in my hand, and the white man's tender heart in my breast, I returned to my own people.

Wearing a foreigner's dress, I walked, a stranger, into my father's village.

Asking my way, for I had not forgotten my native tongue, an old man led me toward the tepee where my father lay. From my old companion I learned that my father had been sick many moons. As we drew near the tepee, I heard the chanting of a medicine-man within it. At once I wished to enter in and drive from my home the sorcerer of the plains, but the old warrior checked me. "Ho, wait outside until the medicine-man leaves your father," he said. While talking he scanned me from head to feet. Then he retraced his steps toward the heart of the camping-ground.

My father's dwelling was on the outer limits of the round-faced village. With every heart-throb I grew more impatient to enter the wigwam.

While I turned the leaves of my Bible with nervous fingers, the medicine-man came forth from the dwelling and walked hurriedly away. His head and face were closely covered with the loose robe which draped his entire figure.

He was tall and large. His long strides I have never forgot. They seemed to me then the uncanny gait of eternal death. Quickly pocketing my Bible, I went into the tepee.

Upon a mat lay my father, with furrowed face and gray hair. His eyes and cheeks were sunken far into his head. His sallow skin lay thin upon his pinched nose and high cheek-bones. Stooping over him, I took his fevered hand. "How, Ate?" I greeted him. A light flashed from his listless eyes and his dried lips parted. "My son!" he murmured, in a feeble voice. Then again the wave of joy and recognition receded. He closed his eyes, and his hand dropped from my open palm to the ground.

Looking about, I saw an old woman sitting with bowed head. Shaking hands with her, I recognized my mother. I sat down between my father and mother as I used to do, but I did not feel at home. The place where my old grandmother used to sit was now unoccupied. With my mother I bowed my head. Alike our throats were choked and tears were streaming from our eyes; but far apart in spirit our ideas and faiths separated us. My grief was for the soul unsaved; and I thought my mother wept to see a brave man's body broken by sickness.

Useless was my attempt to change the faith in the medicine-man to that abstract power named God. Then one day I became righteously mad with anger that the medicine-man should thus ensnare my father's soul. And when he came to chant his sacred songs I pointed toward the door and bade him go! The man's eyes glared upon me for an instant. Slowly gathering his robe about him, he turned his back upon the sick man and stepped out of our wigwam. "Ha, ha, ha! my son, I cannot live without the medicine-man!" I heard my father cry when the sacred man was gone.

III.

On a bright day, when the winged seeds of the prairie-grass were flying hither and thither, I walked solemnly toward the center of the camping-ground. My heart beat hard and irregularly at my side. Tighter I grasped the sacred book I carried under my arm. Now was the beginning of life's work.

Though I knew it would be hard, I did not once feel that failure was to be my reward. As I stepped unevenly on the rolling ground, I thought of the warriors soon to wash off their war-paints and follow me.

At length I reached the place where the people had assembled to hear me preach. In a large circle men and women sat upon the dry red grass. Within the ring I stood, with the white man's Bible in my hand. I tried to tell them of the soft heart of Christ.

In silence the vast circle of bareheaded warriors sat under an afternoon sun. At last, wiping the wet from my brow, I took my place in the ring. The hush of the assembly filled me with great hope.

I was turning my thoughts upward to the sky in gratitude, when a stir called me to earth again.

A tall, strong man arose. His loose robe hung in folds over his right shoulder. A pair of snapping black eyes fastened themselves like the poisonous fangs of a serpent upon me. He was the medicine-man. A tremor played about my heart and a chill cooled the fire in my veins.

Scornfully he pointed a long forefinger in my direction and asked,

"What loyal son is he who, returning to his father's people, wears a foreigner's dress?" He paused a moment, and then continued: "The dress of that foreigner of whom a story says he bound a native of our land, and heaping dry sticks around him, kindled a fire at his feet!" Waving his hand toward me, he exclaimed, "Here is the traitor to his people!"

I was helpless. Before the eyes of the crowd the cunning magician turned my honest heart into a vile nest of treachery. Alas! the people frowned as they looked upon me.

"Listen!" he went on. "Which one of you who have eyed the young man can see through his bosom and warn the people of the nest of young snakes hatching there? Whose ear was so acute that he caught the hissing of snakes whenever the young man opened his mouth? This one has not only proven false to you, but even to the Great Spirit who made him. He is a fool! Why do you sit here giving ear to a foolish man who could not defend his people because he fears to kill, who could not bring venison to renew the life of his sick father? With his prayers, let him drive away the enemy! With his soft heart, let him keep off starvation! We shall go elsewhere to dwell upon an untainted ground."

With this he disbanded the people. When the sun lowered in the west and the winds were quiet, the village of cone-shaped tepees was gone. The medicine-man had won the hearts of the people.

Only my father's dwelling was left to mark the fighting-ground.

IV.

From a long night at my father's bedside I came out to look upon the morning. The yellow sun hung equally between the snow-covered land and the cloudless blue sky. The light of the new day was cold. The strong breath of winter crusted the snow and fitted crystal shells over the rivers and lakes. As I stood in front of the tepee, thinking of the vast prairies which separated us from our tribe, and wondering if the high sky likewise separated the soft-hearted Son of God from us, the icy blast from the North blew through my hair and skull. My neglected hair had grown long and fell upon my neck.

My father had not risen from his bed since the day the medicine-man led the people away. Though I read from the Bible and prayed beside him upon my knees, my father would not listen. Yet I believed my prayers were not unheeded in heaven.

"Ha, ha, ha! my son," my father groaned upon the first snowfall. "My son, our food is gone. There is no one to bring me meat! My son, your soft heart has unfitted you for everything!" Then covering his face with the buffalo-robe, he said no more. Now while I stood out in that cold winter morning, I was starving. For two days I had not seen any food. But my own cold and hunger did not harass my soul as did the whining cry of the sick old man.

Stepping again into the tepee, I untied my snow-shoes, which were fastened to the tent-poles.

My poor mother, watching by the sick one, and faithfully heaping wood upon the center fire, spoke to me:

"My son, do not fail again to bring your father meat, or he will starve to death."

"How, Ina," I answered, sorrowfully. From the tepee I started forth again to hunt food for my aged parents. All day I tracked the white level lands in vain. Nowhere, nowhere were there any other footprints but my own! In the evening of this third fast-day I came back without meat. Only a bundle of sticks for the fire I brought on my back. Dropping the wood outside, I lifted the door-flap and set one foot within the tepee.

There I grew dizzy and numb. My eyes swam in tears. Before me lay my old gray-haired father sobbing like a child. In his horny hands he clutched the buffalo-robe, and with his teeth he was gnawing off the edges. Chewing the dry stiff hair and buffalo-skin, my father's eyes sought my hands. Upon seeing them empty, he cried out:

"My son, your soft heart will let me starve before you bring me meat! Two hills eastward stand a herd of cattle. Yet you will see me die before you bring me food!"

Leaving my mother lying with covered head upon her mat, I rushed out into the night.

With a strange warmth in my heart and swiftness in my feet, I climbed over the first hill, and soon the second one. The moon-light upon the white country showed me a clear path to the white man's cattle. With my hand upon the knife in my belt, I leaned heavily against the fence while counting the herd.

Twenty in all I numbered. From among them I chose the best-fattened creature. Leaping over the fence, I plunged my knife into it.

My long knife was sharp, and my hands, no more fearful and slow, slashed off choice chunks of warm flesh. Bending under the meat I had taken for my starving father, I hurried across the prairie.

Toward home I fairly ran with the life-giving food I carried upon my back. Hardly had I climbed the second hill when I heard sounds coming after me. Faster and faster I ran with my load for my father, but the sounds were gaining upon me. I heard the clicking of snowshoes and the squeaking of the leather straps at my heels; yet I did not turn to see what pursued me, for I was intent upon reaching my father. Suddenly like thunder an angry voice shouted curses and threats into my ear! A rough hand wrenched my shoulder and took the meat from me! I stopped struggling to run. A deafening whir filled my head. The moon and stars began to move. Now the white prairie was sky, and the stars lay under my feet. Now again they were turning. At last the starry blue rose up into place. The noise in my ears was still. A great quiet filled the air. In my hand I found my long knife dripping with blood. At my feet a man's figure lay prone in blood-red snow. The horrible scene about me seemed a trick of my senses, for I could not understand it was real. Looking long upon the blood-stained snow, the load of meat for my starving father reached my recognition at last. Quickly I tossed it over my shoulder and started again homeward.

Tired and haunted I reached the door of the wigwam. Carrying the food before me, I entered with it into the tepee.

"Father, here is food!" I cried, as I dropped the meat near my mother. No answer came. Turning about, I beheld my gray-haired father dead! I saw by the unsteady firelight an old gray-haired skeleton lying rigid and stiff.

Out into the open I started, but the snow at my feet became bloody.

V.

On the day after my father's death, having led my mother to the camp of the medicine-man, I gave myself up to those who were searching for the murderer of the paleface.

They bound me hand and foot. Here in this cell I was placed four days ago.

The shrieking winter winds have followed me hither. Rattling the bars, they howl unceasingly: "Your soft heart! your soft heart will see me die before you bring me food!" Hark! something is clanking the chain on the door. It is being opened. From the dark night without a black figure crosses the threshold . . . It is the guard. He comes to warn me of my fate. He tells me that tomorrow I must die. In his stern face I laugh aloud. I do not fear death.

Yet I wonder who shall come to welcome me in the realm of strange sight. Will the loving Jesus grant me pardon and give my soul a soothing sleep? or will my warrior father greet me and receive me as his son? Will my spirit fly upward to a happy heaven? or shall I sink into the bottomless pit, an outcast from a God of infinite love?

Soon, soon I shall know, for now I see the east is growing red. My heart is strong. My face is calm. My eyes are dry and eager for new scenes. My hands hang quietly at my side. Serene and brave, my soul awaits the men to perch me on the gallows for another flight. I go.

THE SINGING BIRD (1925)

John M. Oskison

Oskison was of Cherokee descent, born in Indian Territory (which later became Oklahoma) in 1874. He graduated from Stanford University in 1898 and began publishing short stories. He moved to New York City, where he worked as an editor for a newspaper and magazine, and died in Tulsa in 1947. As for this exciting, densely plotted story, the reader needs to hold tight: it is dotted with odd, struggling phrasings that can make it seem as if Oskison were translating it (e.g., "Cold, passionless men's business Jim and his three companions were busy about now"; "She knew the privilege of her who turned singing bird to savor the preliminary delights of song!"). The title refers to a cuckolding, "she knew that the full-bloods called the deceiving wife a 'singing bird'; with notes to lure others than her mate." The issue of "full-bloods" versus "half-breeds" is a messier theme.

"NOW WE TALK, me and these Kee-too-wah fellows. Old woman, go to bed!"

Thus Jim Blind-Wolfe dismissed his wife, Jennie, who was not old. With the fleetest glancing look he pushed her gently toward the back door of the firelit cabin, one huge outspread hand covering both of her erect shoulders.

Big Jim, old Spring Frog, Panther, and The Miller made up this inner, unofficial council of the Kee-too-wah organization that had met at Jim's cabin. Self-charged with the duty of carrying out the ancient command to maintain amongst the Cherokees the full-blood inheritance of race purity and race ideals, they would discuss an alarming late growth of outlawry in the tribe, an increase in crime due to idleness, drink and certain disturbing white men who had established themselves in the hills. Paradoxically, as they talked and planned secret pressures here and there, they would pass a jug of honest moonshine—but they would drink from it discreetly, lightly, as full-blood gentlemen should!

"Jim," old Spring Frog opened, "I hear my friend say something about that fellow you hit that day at Tahlequah—"

Jim's sudden, loud guffaw interrupted the old man.

"Him!" and Jim's scornful rumble summed up the case of Lovely Daniel, a wild half-breed neighbor.

Smiling at the muffled sound of Jim's laugh, Jennie Blind-Wolfe drew a gay shawl over the thick black hair that made a shining crown for her cleanly modeled head and oval brown face and went across, under the brilliant September starlight, to the out cabin where she was to sleep. It was an inviting pine-log room, pleasantly odorous of drying vegetables and smoked side meat hung from rafters.

She stood for a minute on the solid adz-hewn step listening to the faint, unintelligible murmur of her husband's voice, the occasional comments of the others whom she had left crouched in front of glowing wood embers in the wide stone fireplace; to the music of Spavinaw Creek racing over its rocky bed to Grand River; to the incessant, high-pitched chirring of crickets in the grass, the hysteric repetitions of katydids and the steady clamor of tree frogs yonder at the edge of the clearing.

A maddening sound, this all-night chorus of the little creatures of grass and forest! For ten nights, as she lay beside the relaxed bulk of her giant husband, she had strained her ears in the effort to hear above their din the sound of a horse's tramping at the timber edge and the sound of a man's footsteps coming across the dead grass of the clearing.

"Oh, why don't they stop! Why don't they stop!" she had cried, silently, in an agony of fear. But tonight—

No fear, no resentment of the chirring voices in the grass, the forest clatter; tonight she knew what was to happen. Tonight she would know the shivery terror, the illicit thrill of the singing bird, but she would not be afraid. Lovely Daniel had promised to come to her. Some time before dawn he would come to the edge of the clearing, repeat twice the call of the hoot-owl. He would come to the tiny window of the out cabin, and then—

Lovely had made a wonderful plan, a credit to his half-breed shrewdness, if not to his name! It had been born of his hatred of big Jim Blind-Wolfe and nourished by a growing fever of desire for Jennie. Enough of it he had revealed to Jennie to set her heart pounding, hang a fox-fire glow in her eyes.

She undressed in the streaming light of a moon just past the half and diamond bright stars that laid a brilliant oblong on the floor in front of the open door. Standing on a warm wolf rug beside the wide home-made bed, she stretched her lithe brown body. Then, comfortably relaxed, she recalled the beginning of Lovely's clever plan; a ripple of laughter, soft, enigmatic, rose to her lips.

The beginning dated from a torrid day of midsummer. The Cherokee tribal council was meeting in the box-like brick capitol, set among young oaks in a fenced square. In the shade, on the trampled grass of this capitol square, lounged a knot of councilmen, townsmen, gossips from the hill farms. Jim Blind-Wolfe—huge, smiling, dominating—was of the group, in which also stood Lovely Daniel. Alert, contentious, sharp of tongue, Lovely was sneering at the full-blood gospel that was being preached. Men grew restive under his jeers and mocking flings until at length Jim demanded the word. In slow, measured terms, as became a man of his impressive presence and bull-like voice, he summed up their drawn-out discussion:

"I tell you, Kee-too-wah fellows don't like this lease business. You lease your land to white man, and pretty soon you don't have any land; white man crowd you out! This here country is Eenyan (Indian) country, set aside for Eenyans. We want to keep it always for Eenyans. Such is belief of Kee-too-wahs, and I am Kee-too-wah!"

These were the words Jim repeated when he told Jennie of what followed. He described Lovely Daniel's quick, angry rush toward him, and mimicked his sharp retort:

"Kee-too-wah fellows—hell! They think they run this here country." Jim could not reproduce the sneer that twisted the half-breed's mouth as he went on: "Kee-too-wahs are fools. White man goin' to come anyway. Jim Blind-Wolfe—huh! Biggest dam' fool of all!" He ended with an evil gesture, the sure insult, and Jim's sledge-hammer fist swung smoothly against the side of his head. Lovely's body, lifted by the blow, was flung sprawling. He lay motionless.

"Jim!" cried old Spring Frog, "maybe so you kill that fellow. Bouff!—My God, I don' like."

Jim carried Lovely Daniel across the road to the porch of the National House, while young Hunt ran for Doctor Beavertail. That grave half-breed came, rolled up his sleeves and set to work. His native skill, combined with his medical school knowledge, sufficed to bring Lovely back to consciousness by late afternoon.

Next morning, with the memory of Jim's devastating and widely advertised blow fresh in their minds, the councilmen—after much half jesting and half serious debate—passed a special Act and sent it to Chief Dennis for signature:

"It shall be unlawful for Jim Blind-Wolfe to strike a man with his closed fist!"

It was promptly signed and posted in the corridor of the capitol. Jim read it, and as he strode out into the square the thin line of his sparse mustache was lifted by a loud gust of laughter. Hailing the Chief, fifty yards away, he roared:

"Hey, Dennis, must I only slap that Lovely Daniel fellow next time?" The Chief met him at the center of the square. In an undertone, he undertook a friendly warning:

"You want to watch out for that Daniel fellow, Jim. You mighty nigh killed him, and—I kind of wish you had! He's bad. Bad—" the Chief repeated soberly, and came closer to impress Jim by his words—"We ain't got sure proof yet, but I'm satisfied it was Lovely Daniel that waylaid Blue Logan on the Fort Gibson road and killed him."

The Chief's low-toned confidences went on; and before he mounted the steps and went in to his battered old desk, he recalled:

"You have seen that Yellow Crest woman sometimes? She comes into town from the hills with stovewood and sits on her wagon, with a shawl always across her face. She was a pretty young woman six years ago, wife of Looney Squirrel. This Lovely Daniel took to hanging round, and Looney caught 'em—Yellow Crest and him. You are Kee-too-wah, Jim; you know what the old fellows do to a 'singing bird'?"

"Yes," Jim admitted, "they cut off the end of her nose!"

"Yes, they punish the woman so, and—" the Chief's face showed a shadow of passionate resentment— "they do nothing to the man! The old fellows, the Kee-too-wahs," he repeated, "still do that way. It was what Looney Squirrel did before he sent Yellow Crest from his cabin."

"Yes, I know," Jim assented.

"This Lovely Daniel is bad for women to know; a bad fellow for any woman to know, Jim!" The Chief eyed him shrewdly, pressed his piston-like arm in friendly emphasis before he walked slowly away.

On the long drive to his clearing beside Spavinaw Creek, Jim weighed Chief Dennis' words. He thought of Jennie's fond care of Lovely Daniel's frail sister, Betsy, who was fighting a hopeless battle against tuberculosis in the cabin across the Spavinaw where she lived with Lovely.

"A bad fellow for any woman to know!" Jim repeated, with half closed, contemplative eyes as he urged his tough pony team along the stony road. He would have to think about that. He would have to take more notice of his wife, too—that gay, slender, laughing young woman who kept his cabin, clung adoringly to him, her eyes dancing, and flashed into song with the sudden clear burst of a red bird in early spring—

Lovely as a menace to himself was one thing, he considered; foolishly, he refused to believe that he might be in serious danger from the half-breed; he believed that Lovely was a boaster, a coward, and that he would be afraid of the prompt vengeance of Jim's friends. But Lovely as a menace to Jennie—well, no friend would serve him here, either to warn, fearing his wrath and the tiger-swipe of his great hand, or to avenge!

In direct fashion Jim spoke to Jennie of his encounter with the half-breed, and repeated the Chief's words of warning. A passing gleam of fear rounded her eyes as she listened; it changed to a gay defiant smile when her man added:

"I think you better not go to see Betsy anymore."

"No?" she queried, then very gravely: "she is awful low, Jim, and I am her friend." She sat studying her husband's face for many minutes, turned to the pots hanging in the fireplace with a tiny secret smile. "I am Betsy's best friend," she reiterated coaxingly.

"Well," Jim conceded, stretching his great bulk negligently, "you watch out for that fellow, her brother!"

Some days later, Jennie rode to the capitol, sought Chief Dennis and asked:

"Is Jim in real danger from Lovely Daniel?"

"I think maybe he is in great danger, Jennie; but Jim does not agree with me on that!" The Chief's slow smile was a tribute to her husband's careless bravery.

"Ah, that would make it easier for Lovely," she said to herself softly.

Jennie's thoughts drifted back to various occasions when she had visited Betsy Daniel. Sometimes, but not often, as she sat with her friend or busied herself sweeping and airing the cabin, preparing a bowl of hominy, putting on a pot of greens and bacon, stripping husks from roasting ears, helping on a patchwork quilt, Lovely would come in. He would squat, a thin handsome figure, in front of the fire, sniff eagerly at the cooking pots, rise, move restlessly about. He would speak with Jennie of his hunting; he would talk of the white men he knew at Vinita, some of whom came to the Spavinaw hills in the late fall to chase deer with him and encourage him to become active in tribal politics. These men wished to spur him to active opposition to the reactionary full-bloods, the Kee-too-wahs, who bitterly resented white intrusion.

When Jennie was ready to leave, he would bring her pony to the door, hold his hand for her to step on as she mounted; and he would turn glittering black eyes and grinning face up to her as she gathered the reins to ride away. She had known of Yellow Crest's punishment; she knew that the full-bloods called the deceiving wife a "singing bird," with notes to lure others than her mate; and in Lovely Daniel's eyes she had read an invitation to sing!

When Jim had thrashed the half-breed, she wondered if that invitation would still hold good. The end of her wondering and weighing was a resolve to find out.

Two weeks she waited and planned before riding across Spavinaw Creek, and during that time news of Lovely Daniel drifted to her ears. He had crossed the line into Arkansas with one of the reckless Pigeon boys. They had secured whisky, had rioted in the streets of a border town, had been chased home to the hills by peace officers. The half-breed had brought back a new pistol from Maysville, and up and down the Illinois River and amongst his friends on Flint Creek he had sprinkled ugly threats against Jim. In mid-August, when she knew that he was at home, Jennie rode across to Betsy.

For half an hour, as Jim Blind-Wolfe's wife made Betsy comfortable in a big chair beside the doorway and put the cabin to rights, Lovely sat on the doorstep digging at its worn surface with a pocket knife, saying nothing. Then he disappeared in the brush, to return presently with his saddle-horse. At sunset, after Jennie had cleared away the early supper dishes and tucked Betsy into bed, he was waiting to ride with her. Eyes lowered, fingers nervously caressing her pony's mane, Jennie rode in silence. They crossed Spavinaw at the lonely ford, where she had often seen deer come down to drink, and went slowly up the steep, pine-covered slope. Near Jim's clearing she stopped. Without raising her eyes, she put out her hand.

"Now you go back," she half whispered. "I see you again." Lovely crowded his horse close, took her hand, muttered:

"Look up, Jennie, let me see what is in your eyes!" But she turned her head away and answered:

"I am afraid of you, Lovely—good-by." She pressed his supple, eager fingers, urged her pony forward. He dared not pursue, and turned back; at the ford he whooped, uttering the primitive burst of sound that expressed for him hatred, lust, exultation. His wildcat eyes glowed. Back at his cabin, when he had loosed his hobbled horse to browse in the brush, he sat in the doorway conjuring up pictures of the evil he meant to do Jim Blind-Wolfe and his young and foolish wife. First, he would make Jennie a sinister, branded outcast in the sight of the tribe, and then after Jim had tasted that bitterness he would lay for him. There would be a shot. Someone would find him, a stiffening corpse, beside a lonely road! Until long after the new moon had sunk he sat, at times crooning fragments of old Cherokee songs, or flinging an occasional gay word to Betsy.

At Jennie's next visit, Betsy sent her brother to the Eucha settlement store for medicine. He had scarcely gone when Betsy called Jennie to her side, looking searchingly into her face.

"You are very dear to me, Jennie," she said in Cherokee, her hand stroking the other's face, fever-glowing eyes and a stain of tell-tale red on her thin cheeks emphasizing her anxiety. "Will you promise me that you will be wise, and careful—with Lovely? I do not want to lose you for the little time left to me!"

Jennie put her arm about her friend's wasted shoulders and leaned to whisper:

"My sister, you will not lose me."

"But Lovely—he is wild—he is Jim Blind-Wolfe's enemy—and I am afraid." Her words were hesitant, but suggestive.

"You are my friend," Jennie assured her quickly. "What I do will be best for both of us—and Lovely too! You will trust me?"

Betsy nodded, fell quiet under Jennie's gentle caresses.

Again Lovely rode across the ford with Jennie, rode close, begging for the promise that seemed to hang upon her lips; and before they parted she gave it, in a soft rush of speech:

"That will be hard, what you ask, Lovely, but some time when Jim is not with me I will let you know!" The half-breed's whoop at the ford punctuated a snatch of song.

Jennie was committed now. She quieted Jim's vague uneasiness at her visits to the cabin, by emphasizing Betsy's need of her care and asserting that Lovely's behavior was correct. By cunning degrees, she led the half-breed to reveal his plan for squaring accounts with her husband—that is, the part involving Jim's assassination. To Lovely's passionate outburst of hate she replied crooningly:

"Yes, I know. He hurt you, Lovely!"

By late August, when dying summer had released upon the night myriad insect sounds, above whose clamorous fiddling and chirring casual noises were hard to distinguish, she had stirred Lovely to a very frenzy of impatience. More than the desire of vengeance drew him now. He wanted Jennie for herself. He had sworn to come to her when the new moon was as wide, at the center of its crescent, as the red ribbon that bound her hair. He would come to the edge of the clearing some time before dawn— Jim would be asleep—and twice he would utter the hoot-owl's cry. She must slip out to him. If she did not, he swore that he would cross the clearing cat-footedly, open the door very slowly and quietly, come in and shoot Jim as he lay asleep. And then—

"Oh, no, not blood!" she cried, fighting desperately to alter his determination. He raved, boasted. She held out, pleading:

"No, no, not blood, in my sight! Wait until I come to you." As he persisted, she threatened: "If I hear you coming to the door, I will scream and Jim will rise up and kill you!"

Night after night she lay, sleeping fitfully, listening for the double owl cry, straining her ears to catch, above the high-pitched monotone of the insects' singing, the sound of footsteps in the dead grass. Twice during that time of waiting she visited Betsy and fought off Lovely's importunate advances with the warning:

"It must be safe—no blood. I will let you know."

The moon had filled its crescent, was swelling to fullness, before the opportunity Jennie had waited for arrived. Then Jim told her of the coming secret council in his cabin of the leaders of the Kee-too-wahs. They would eat supper and talk all night. She would prepare a pot of coffee for them, set it beside the fire and go to sleep in the out cabin. She weighed the peril, decided, and slipped across to Spavinaw to tell Lovely Daniel:

"Come to the out cabin before dawn, as you have said. Come to the little window that looks toward the creek. Tap, and I will open and say if all is safe." In a quick upward glance from her lowered eyes, Jennie saw the half-breed's grin of triumph. Trembling, she sent him back to the ford and his whooping rush up the opposite slope. In his eyes she had read—love of her? Yes; and death for Jim! Lovely's hatred of the giant who had all but killed him with a blow of his fist had become a crackling blaze in his breast.

Ten days of strain and nights of broken sleep had fined the edges of Jennie's nerves. She lay quite wide awake now, certain of herself, confident; and now she did not care about the foolish insect noises. She leaned out of bed to place her deerskin slippers at just the spot she desired to have them and hang a warm shawl over a chair where she could seize it with one movement of her hand. Fingers clasped behind her head, she lay watching a little square of starlit and moonlit sky through the window.

A rooster's crowing announced midnight; a little later she heard Jim's heavy step on the east porch of the main cabin as he emerged to sniff the fresh air, and then the slam of the door as he went in; she was aware of the pleasantly nipping coolness of the period before daybreak; again there was a stir on the east porch.

Cold, passionless men's business Jim and his three companions were busy about now. Impersonal, free from individual angers, jealousies, attachments, they sat, like remote, secret gods, in judgment on the conduct of a community, the policy of a tribe. Kee-too-wah tradition, the old conception of tribal integrity, the clean spirit of ancestors who had successfully fought against race deterioration and the decay of morale in the long years of contact with the whites in Georgia and Tennessee—these were their preoccupations. They harked back to legendary days, to the very beginning, when the Great Spirit had handed over to the tribe a sacred fire, with the injunction to keep it burning forever; and they strove to keep alive in the minds of an easy living, careless generation the memory of that road of Calvary over which their fathers and mothers had been driven when the then new Indian country was settled.

Jennie could understand but vaguely the purpose which dominated the four. It seemed shadowy, very different from the flaming, heart-stirring enterprise that concerned her! She lay taut-strung, like a bow made ready, thinking, feeling. Soon now, perhaps when the talk in the cabin had thinned and sleep was close to the eyelids of the four, she would hear a tapping at the window. She began to listen, to watch for a shadow at the little opening.

It came. Lovely's head and shoulders made a blur against the small luminous square; his tapping was as light as the flick of a bird's wing, insistent as the drumming of the male partridge in spring. Jennie stepped into her slippers, flung the shawl about her shoulders, flitted silently to the window.

She would not let him in at once. She knew the steps which she must take in order to test his ardor, stir him to impetuous frenzy. She knew the privilege of her who turned singing bird to savor the preliminary delights of song! She pushed the tiny sliding window aside a crack and whispered:

"Who has come?" At Lovely's fatuous answer, she laughed a faint ghost laugh and breathed: "Why have you come?" Then, before he could speak, "no, don't tell me; wait and let me talk with you here for a time."

In throaty whispers, only half coherent, the man pressed his suit. Jennie went silent in the midst of his jumbled speeches, so stirred by inner turmoil that she scarcely heard his pleading. Then her trembling voice insisted:

"You must wait a little while longer, Lovely. I am afraid. But I will let you come in before it is light. I promise!" Her shawl was drawn across her face, and as she put timid fingers in his reaching hand he felt them shake. Again, in maddening repetition, she sang the refrain:

"Wait; and tell me once more what it is that you and I will do after tonight. Wait a little. I will not be afraid to let you in after a time." When he threatened to leave the window and go round to the door, she protested in great agitation:

"No, no. The bar is up against you, and if you rattle the door Jim will hear. He will come and spoil everything. He would—" her voice all but faded in her throat—"he would kill you, Lovely!"

★ ★ ★

At length the last note of the singing bird had been sounded, and Jennie answered to Lovely's frantic entreaty:

"Come now to the door swiftly and silently, in bare feet. Leave your coat there." She pointed, and stood breathless, watching his movements. He dropped shoes, coat, belt and pistol holster in a heap. With a gasp of relief, she ran to unbar the door.

"Quick!" she urged, pulling him into the blinding darkness. Then, close to his ear, "wait for me here!" She flashed by him, stepped through the doorway, closed him in and reached up to trip the stout greased bar that she had prepared. It slid noiselessly across to engage iron stirrups fixed in the heavy door and the massive logs of the door frame. Clasping her shawl tightly about her body, she ran to the cabin where Jim and his three friends sat in silence, cross-legged in front of the fireplace. She opened the door and called:

"Jim!" He jerked his head up, rose. "Don't be troubled," she told the others. "Jim will be back soon." She shut the door as the great bulk of her husband emerged.

"Quick, Jim, come with me." She seized his big paw and dragged at it. "Quick! quick!" He followed at a lumbering trot, dazed and uttering fragments of questions. To the back of the out cabin she led him, ran to the dark heap of Lovely Daniel's clothes, seized belt, holster and pistol and thrust them into Jim's hands.

"Here, what's this!" he bellowed. Inside there was the sound of bare feet rushing across the floor, an ineffectual yank at the door, a snarl of disappointed rage—then silence.

"Jim!" His wife was on tiptoe in the effort to bring her lips nearer to his ear.

"In there is Lovely Daniel. He came to kill you, Jim.—Listen, Jim: he came to kill you, do you understand? I knew why he was coming and I—I made him believe I was a—a singing bird, Jim! And he came to me first.—But I did not, Jim—I put down the outside bar that I had fixed, as soon as he came in, and ran to you. —Come and see. Come and see how I fixed it." She pulled him round to the door, showed him the bar firm in its place. "See, I fixed it so to trap him. You see, Jim?"

A faint glimmer of daylight had come, and big Jim stooped to look into the shining eyes of his wife. His gaze was like a down-thrust knife, cutting clean and deep into her soul. It found there only a turbulent fear for him, a sunburst of adoration that excited in him a surge of primitive joy. He came erect.

"Ah, you Lovely Daniel!" he shouted savagely. "You try to make singing bird out of my wife!" He broke into the old Cherokee killer's dread warning, the wild turkey's gobble.

With his hand on the door, and before he could lift the bar, he saw his friends emerge from the main cabin. Old Spring Frog peered round the corner from the east porch. He had heard the turkey gobbler signal! Jim thought swiftly; these men must not know that Lovely Daniel was in the out cabin, where his wife had slept. In a voice forced to calmness, he called to Spring Frog:

"I just now hear a big old gobbler, yonder." He pointed across the clearing toward the creek. The three returned to their places in front of the fire.

Jim flung up the outer bar, swung the door wide and struck aside the knife-armed hand that leaped toward his breast. The weapon dropped, and Jim grabbed Lovely by the shirt to drag him forth.

"Put on your clothes," he ordered. With one hand helpless from the force of Jim's blow, the half-breed made slow progress with his dressing, and Jim had time to think, to make a little plan of his own. With shawl drawn closely about her body and over her head, Jennie stood waiting at the corner of the out cabin, watching the dawn change from gray to pink-shot silver.

Dressed, Lovely Daniel stood still, in a sort of frozen apathy, awaiting he wondered what terrible retribution. Jim grasped his arm, turned his head to speak to Jennie:

"Stay in here until I come." She disappeared into the shadowy cabin, closed the door, ran to crouch against the thick pillow and the rude headboard of the bed—and waited.

Jim led the half-breed round to the east porch of the main cabin, opened the door and thrust him into view of his friends. They looked up, curious, expectant.

"Ah," muttered old Spring Frog, "I did hear what I heard!"— Jim's warning gobble.

"This fellow—" Jim shoved Lovely Daniel close to the cross-legged group—"come to kill me. My wife, she hear him coming and she run to tell me just now." He fell silent, waited for a minute, then:

"You know this fellow, what I done to him. You know this fellow, how he kill Blue Logan, how he make Yellow Crest outcast woman, how he make Looney Squirrel a man ashamed. —We get rid of this fellow?" The last words were more a statement than a question, but his friends nodded assent.

"Let that be done," old Spring Frog, staunch Kee-too-wah defender of Indian probity, made a sign; it was repeated by Panther and The Miller. The three rose to stand beside Jim Blind-Wolfe.

Sure of his friends now, Jim's face framed a smile, a kind of savage radiance. He spoke rapidly for a minute, reached for the brown whisky jug that was a blob of darkness on the wide, lighted hearth—the jug from which the four had drunk sparingly throughout the night. Still smiling, he handed it to the half-breed.

"This fellow like whisky—drink!" Lovely Daniel took the jug, tilted it and drank deep, the Adam's apple in his lean throat working rhythmically as he gulped the raw, hot liquor. When at last he removed the jug from his lips he shook it to show how little remained. They would not say that he had been afraid to drink! Jim's smile turned to a low laugh as he spoke to his friends:

"I take this fellow outside now; you wait here for me few minutes."

The two stepped out to the east porch, facing a fast-mounting radiance that presaged the coming of sunrise. Jim carried the half-breed's pistol. He led Lovely Daniel to the end of the porch; they stood in silence, Jim's eyes fixed on the other's face. At the edge of the clearing they heard a crow's awakening "caw! caw!" and the jarring call of a jaybird.

Jim spoke musingly, earnestly:

"Listen, Lovely Daniel: If you want to do that, you can go away from here—clear away from all Cherokee people, and I will not kill you!" Jim's stunning speech hung suspended, and Lovely's eyes sought his face; he resumed: "If you go away, it must be for all time. You must be outcast always. You try to come back, Kee-too-wah will know and I will then kill you. You know that?" The other nodded somberly. Jim spoke again, his gaze boring into eyes that wavered: "But I don't think you want to go away, like that, to stay always, lost man. Well, then?

"Listen: I will tell you one other way. Like this, Lovely Daniel—you can go up yonder, if you are brave man—"solemnly Jim pointed to the crimson-streaked sky—"on the back of the sun! Old Cherokee folks tell about how Eenyans go home to Great

Spirit on the back of the sun. I don't know; maybe so; you can try.
—You try?" His face had become stern now, and menacing; he
bent close to peer into the drink-flushed face of the half-breed.

Lovely Daniel weighed the alternatives swiftly. Reeling, aflame
with the fiery liquid he had drunk, his mind seized upon Jim's
suggestion.

"I go with the sun!" he cried, swaying toward the edge of the
porch. Boastfully, exultantly, he demanded, "Give me my gun."
Jim handed him the pistol, stepped backwards noiselessly, his eyes
holding Lovely. His hand on the latch, he stopped.

Lovely Daniel's uninjured hand, loosely gripping the pistol, hung
at his side as he watched the full daylight spread down to the edge
of the clearing. Out of some deep, long-hidden spring of memory
rose a fragment of wild song, a chant of death. It mounted to a
fervid burst, as the sharp red edge of the sun appeared; it ended in
a triumphant whoop—and the roar of the pistol, pressed against his
temple, sent a perching crow whirling upwards with a startled
"caw!"

Jim stepped inside.

"What was that?" Spring Frog questioned perfunctorily.

"Lovely Daniel was making answer," Jim responded
enigmatically.

"Making answer? To what?"

"Oh, a singing bird, I think—early morning singing bird, I
think." He looked into the faces of his friends until he knew that
they understood, then turned to go out. He lingered to say:

"If you fellows go look out for that which was Lovely Daniel, I
get my wife to come and cook breakfast for us."

He found Jennie still crouched on the bed, hands still clapped
tight against her ears. He gathered her into his arms, a vast tenderness and a fierce pride in her courage thrilling through him. With
her face buried beneath his cheek and her arms tight about his
neck, he sat on the bed and whispered:

"All is well now, all is!" Her convulsive hold on him
tightened.

"Oh, my Jim!" she breathed fiercely and, after a minute, "I can
go now and care for Betsy without fear."

"Yes." Jim's eyes sought the brilliant oblong of daylight that was
the doorway, and his voice was tender and solemn as he added:

"You can go to Betsy now, and tell her that Lovely went home without fear, on the back of the sun. I think she will understand what you say. —Pretty soon you come and cook breakfast?"

"Pretty soon I come," she echoed and, shivering, settled even closer to the great bulk of her husband.

TRAIN TIME (1936)

D'Arcy McNickle

The ethnographic anthropologist D'Arcy McNickle, whose ancestry was Salish-Kootenai and Cree, was born on the Flathead Reservation in Montana in 1904. He worked as a staff member under John Collier, commissioner of the U.S. government's Bureau of Indian Affairs, and later directed the Newberry Library in Chicago's Center for American Indian History. In the 1960s he was chairperson of the Anthropology Department at the University of Saskatchewan in Regina. His quiet and intense stories seem to have been informed by a deep experience of Chekhov's and Hemingway's short fiction. McNickle died in 1977.

On the depot platform everybody stood waiting, listening. The train had just whistled, somebody said. They stood listening and gazing eastward, where railroad tracks and creek emerged together from a tree-chocked canyon.

Twenty-five boys, five girls, Major Miles—all stood waiting and gazing eastward. Was it true that the train had whistled?

"That was no train!" a boy's voice explained.

"It was a steer bellowing."

"It was the train!"

Girls crowded backward against the station building, heads hanging, tears starting; boys pushed forward to the edge of the platform. An older boy with a voice already turning heavy stepped off the weather-shredded boardwalk and stood wide-legged in the middle of the track. He was the doubter. He had heard no train.

Major Miles boomed. "You! What's your name? Get back here! Want to get killed? All of you, stand back!"

The Major strode about, soldier-like, and waved commands. He was exasperated. He was tired. A man driving cattle through

40

timber had it easy, he was thinking. An animal trainer had no idea of trouble. Let anyone try corralling twenty-thirty Indian kids, dragging them out of hiding places, getting them away from relatives and together in one place, then holding them, without tying them, until train time! Even now, at the last moment, when his worries were almost over, they were trying to get themselves killed!

Major Miles was a man of conscience. Whatever he did, he did earnestly. On this hot end-of-summer day he perspired and frowned and wore his soldier bearing. He removed his hat from his wet brow and thoughtfully passed his hand from the hair line backward. Words tumbled about in his mind. Somehow, he realized, he had to vivify the moment. These children were about to go out from the Reservation and get a new start. Life would change. They ought to realize it, somehow—

"Boys—and girls—" There were five girls, he remembered. He had got them all lined up against the building, safely away from the edge of the platform. The air was stifling with end-of-the-summer heat. It was time to say something, never mind the heat. Yes, he would have to make the moment real. He stood soldier-like and thought that.

"Boys and girls—" The train whistled, dully, but unmistakably. Then it repeated more clearly. The rails came to life, something was running through them and making them sing.

Just then the Major's eye fell upon little Eneas and his sure voice faltered. He knew about little Eneas. Most of the boys and girls were mere names; he had seen them around the Agency with their parents or had caught sight of them scurrying around behind tepees and barns when he visited their homes. But little Eneas he knew. With him before his eyes, he paused.

He remembered so clearly the winter day, six months ago, when he first saw Eneas. It was the boy's grandfather, Michel Lamartine, he had gone to see. Michel had contracted to cut wood for the Agency but had not started work. The Major had gone to discover why not.

It was the coldest day of the winter, late in February, and the cabin, sheltered as it was among the pine and cottonwood of a creek bottom, was shot through by frosty drafts. There was wood all about them. Lamartine was a woodcutter besides, yet there was no wood in the house. The fire in the flat-topped cast-iron stove burned weakly. The reason was apparent. The Major had but to look at the bed where Lamartine lay, twisted and shrunken by rheumatism. Only his black eyes burned with life. He tried to wave a hand as the Major entered.

"You see how I am!" the gesture indicated. Then a nerve-strung voice faltered. "We have it bad here. My old woman, she's not much good."

Clearly she wasn't, not for wood-chopping. She sat close by the fire, trying with a good natured grin to lift her ponderous body from a low-seated rocking chair. The Major had to motion her back to her ease. She breathed with asthmatic roar. Wood-chopping was not within her range. With only a squaw's hatchet to work with, she could scarcely have come within striking distance of a stick of wood. Two blows, if she had struck them, might have put a stop to her laboring heart.

"You see how it is," Lamartine's eyes flashed.

The Major saw clearly. Sitting there in the frosty cabin, he pondered their plight and wondered if he could get away without coming down with pneumonia. A stream of wind seemed to be hitting him in the back of the neck. Of course, there was nothing to do. One saw too many such situations. If one undertook to provide sustenance out of one's own pocket there would be no end to the demands. Government salaries were small, resources were limited. He could do no more than shake his head sadly, offer some vague hope, some small sympathy. He would have to get away at once.

Then a hand fumbled at the door; it opened. After a moment's struggle, little Eneas appeared, staggering under a full armload of pine limbs hacked into short lengths. The boy was no taller than an ax handle, his nose was running, and he had a croupy cough. He dropped the wood into the empty box near the old woman's chair, then straightened himself.

A soft chuckling came from the bed. Lamartine was full of pride. "A good boy, that. He keeps the old folks warm."

Something about the boy made the Major forget his determination to depart. Perhaps it was his wordlessness, his uncomplaining wordlessness. Or possibly it was his loyalty to the old people. Something drew his eyes to the boy and set him to thinking. Eneas was handing sticks of wood to the old woman and she was feeding them into the stove. When the fire box was full a good part of the boy's armload was gone. He would have to cut more, and more, to keep the old people warm.

The Major heard himself saying suddenly, "Sonny, show me your woodpile. Let's cut a lot of wood for the old folks."

It happened just like that, inexplicably. He went even farther. Not only did he cut enough wood to last through several days, but when he had finished he put the boy in the Agency car and drove him to town, five miles there and back. Against his own principles, he bought a week's worth of groceries, and excused himself by telling the boy, as they drove homeward, "Your grandfather won't be able to get to town for a few days yet. Tell him to come see me when he gets well."

That was the beginning of the Major's interest in Eneas. He had decided that day that he would help the boy in any way possible, because he was a boy of quality. You would be shirking your duty if you failed to recognize and to help a boy of his sort. The only question was, how to help?

When he saw the boy again, some weeks later, his mind saw the problem clearly. "Eneas," he said, "I'm going to help you. I'll see that the old folks are taken care of, so you won't have to think about them. Maybe the old man won't have rheumatism next year, anyhow. If he does, I'll find a family where he and the old lady can move in and be looked after. Don't worry about them. Just think about yourself and what I'm going to do for you. Eneas, when it comes school time, I'm going to send you away. How do you like that?" The Major smiled at his own happy idea.

There was silence. No shy smiling, no look of gratitude, only silence. Probably he had not understood.

"You understand, Eneas? Your grandparents will be taken care of. You'll go away and learn things. You'll go on a train."

The boy looked here and there and scratched at the ground with his foot. "Why do I have to go away?"

"You don't have to, Eneas. Nobody will make you. I thought you'd like to. I thought—" The Major paused, confused.

"You won't make me go away, will you?" There was fear in the voice, tears threatening.

"Why, no, Eneas. If you don't want to go. I thought—"

The Major dropped the subject. He didn't see the boy again through the spring and summer, but he thought of him. In fact, he couldn't forget the picture he had of him that first day. He couldn't forget either that he wanted to help him. Whether the boy understood what was good for him or not, he meant to see to it that the right thing was done. And that was why, when he made up a quota of children to be sent to the school in Oregon, the name of Eneas Lamartine was included. The Major did not discuss it with him again, but he set the wheels in motion. The boy would go with the others. In time to come, he would understand. Possibly he would be grateful.

Thirty children were included in the quota, and of them all Eneas was the only one the Major had actual knowledge of, the only one in whom he was personally interested. With each of them, it was true, he had had difficulties. None had wanted to go. They said they "liked it at home," or they were "afraid" to go away, or they would "get sick" in a strange country; and the parents were no help. They too were frightened and uneasy. It was a tiresome, hard kind of duty, but the Major knew what was required of him and never hesitated. The difference was, that in the cases of all these others, the problem was routine. He met it, and passed over it. But in the case of Eneas, he was bothered. He wanted to make clear what this moment of going away meant. It was a breaking away from fear and doubt and ignorance. Here began the new. Mark it, remember it.

His eyes lingered on Eneas. There he stood, drooping, his nose running as on that first day, his stockings coming down, his jacket in need of buttons. But under that shabbiness, the Major knew, was a real quality. There was a boy who, with the right help, would blossom and grow strong. It was important that he should not go away hurt and resentful.

The Major called back his straying thoughts and cleared his throat. The moment was important.

"Boys and girls—"

The train was pounding near. Already it had emerged from the canyon and momently the headlong flying locomotive loomed blacker and larger. A white plume flew upward—Whoo-oo, whoo-oo.

The Major realized in sudden remorse that he had waited too long. A vital moment had come, and he had paused, looked for words, and lost it. The roar of rolling steel was upon them.

Lifting his voice in desperate haste, his eyes fastened on Eneas, he bellowed, "Boys and girls—be good—"

That was all anyone heard.

THE MAN TO SEND RAIN CLOUDS
(1969)

Leslie Marmon Silko

Born in 1948 in New Mexico, of Laguna Pueblo ancestry, Silko published "The Man to Send Rain Clouds" while an undergraduate at the University of New Mexico. The poet and novelist has taught at the University of Arizona, the University of New Mexico, and Emory University. "The reason I write," she remarked in an interview, "is to find out what I mean. I know some of the things I mean. I couldn't tell you the best things I know. And I can't know the best things I know until I write."[1]

THEY FOUND HIM under a big cottonwood tree. His Levi jacket and pants were faded light-blue so that he had been easy to find. The big cottonwood tree stood apart from a small grove of winterbare cottonwoods which grew in the wide, sandy, arroyo. He had been dead for a day or more, and the sheep had wandered and scattered up and down the arroyo. Leon and his brother-in-law, Ken, gathered the sheep and left them in the pen at the sheep camp before they returned to the cottonwood tree. Leon waited under the tree while Ken drove the truck through the deep sand to the edge of the arroyo. He squinted up at the sun and unzipped his jacket. It sure was hot for this time of year. But high and northwest the blue mountains were still deep in snow. Ken came sliding down the low, crumbling bank about fifty yards down, and he was bringing the red blanket.

---

1. Laura Coltelli. *Winged Words: American Indian Writers Speak.* Lincoln: University of Nebraska Press. 1990. 151.

Before they wrapped the old man, Leon took a piece of string out of his pocket and tied a small gray feather in the old man's long white hair. Ken gave him the paint. Across the brown wrinkled forehead he drew a streak of white and along the high cheekbones he drew a strip of blue paint. He paused and watched Ken throw pinches of corn meal and pollen into the wind that fluttered the small gray feather. Then Leon painted with yellow under the old man's broad nose, and finally, when he had painted green across the chin, he smiled.

"Send us rain clouds, Grandfather." They laid the bundle in the back of the pickup and covered it with a heavy tarp before they started back to the pueblo.

They turned off the highway onto the sandy pueblo road. Not long after they passed the store and post office they saw Father Paul's car coming toward them. When he recognized their faces he slowed his car and waved for them to stop. The young priest rolled down the car window.

"Did you find old Teofilo?" he asked loudly.

Leon stopped the truck. "Good morning, Father. We were just out to the sheep camp. Everything is O.K. now."

"Thank God for that. Teofilo is a very old man. You really shouldn't allow him to stay at the sheep camp alone."

"No, he won't do that any more now."

"Well, I'm glad you understand. I hope I'll be seeing you at Mass this week. We missed you last Sunday. See if you can get old Teofilo to come with you." The priest smiled and waved at them as they drove away.

Louise and Teresa were waiting. The table was set for lunch, and the coffee was boiling on the black iron stove. Leon looked at Louise and then at Teresa.

"We found him under a cottonwood tree in the big arroyo near sheep camp. I guess he sat down to rest in the shade and never got up again." Leon walked toward the old man's bed. The red plaid shawl had been shaken and spread carefully over the bed, and a new brown flannel shirt and pair of stiff new Levis were arranged neatly beside the pillow. Louise held the screen door open while Leon and Ken carried in the red blanket. He looked small and shriveled, and after they dressed him in the new shirt and pants he seemed more shrunken.

It was noontime now because the church bells rang the Angelus. They ate the beans with hot bread, and nobody said anything until after Teresa poured the coffee.

Ken stood up and put on his jacket. "I'll see about the gravediggers. Only the top layer of soil is frozen. I think it can be ready before dark."

Leon nodded his head and finished his coffee. After Ken had been gone for a while, the neighbors and clanspeople came quietly to embrace Teofilo's family and to leave food on the table because the gravediggers would come to eat when they were finished.

The sky in the west was full of pale-yellow light. Louise stood outside with her hands in the pockets of Leon's green army jacket that was too big for her. The funeral was over, and the old men had taken their candles and medicine bags and were gone. She waited until the body was laid into the pickup before she said anything to Leon. She touched his arm, and he noticed that her hands were still dusty from the corn meal that she had sprinkled around the old man. When she spoke, Leon could not hear her.

"What did you say? I didn't hear you."

"I said that I had been thinking about something."

"About what?"

"About the priest sprinkling holy water for Grandpa. So he won't be thirsty."

Leon stared at the new moccasins that Teofilo had made for the ceremonial dances in the summer. They were nearly hidden by the red blanket. It was getting colder, and the wind pushed gray dust down the narrow pueblo road. The sun was approaching the long mesa where it disappeared during the winter. Louise stood there shivering and watching his face. Then he zipped up his jacket and opened the truck door. "I'll see if he's there."

Ken stopped the pickup at the church, and Leon got out; and then Ken drove down the hill to the graveyard where people were waiting. Leon knocked at the old carved door with its symbols of the Lamb. While he waited he looked up at the twin bells from the king of Spain with the last sunlight pouring around them in their tower.

The priest opened the door and smiled when he saw who it was. "Come in! What brings you here this evening?"

The priest walked toward the kitchen, and Leon stood with his cap in his hand, playing with the earflaps and examining the living room, the brown sofa, the green armchair, and the brass lamp that hung down from the ceiling by links of chain. The priest dragged a chair out of the kitchen and offered it to Leon.

"No thank you, Father. I only came to ask you if you would bring your holy water to the graveyard."

The priest turned away from Leon and looked out the window at the patio full of shadows and the dining-room windows of the nuns' cloister across the patio. The curtains were heavy, and the light from within faintly penetrated; it was impossible to see the nuns inside eating supper. "Why didn't you tell me he was dead? I could have brought the Last Rites anyway."

Leon smiled. "It wasn't necessary, Father."

The priest stared down at his scuffed brown loafers and the worn hem of his cassock. "For a Christian burial it was necessary."

His voice was distant, and Leon thought that his blue eyes looked tired.

"It's O.K., Father, we just want him to have plenty of water."

The priest sank down into the green chair and picked up a glossy missionary magazine. He turned the colored pages full of lepers and pagans without looking at them.

"You know I can't do that, Leon. There should have been the Last Rites and a funeral Mass at the very least."

Leon put on his green cap and pulled the flaps down over his ears. "It's getting late, Father. I've got to go."

When Leon opened the door Father Paul stood up and said, "Wait." He left the room and came back wearing a long brown overcoat. He followed Leon out the door and across the dim churchyard to the adobe steps in front of the church. They both stooped to fit through the low adobe entrance. And when they started down the hill to the graveyard only half of the sun was visible above the mesa.

The priest approached the grave slowly, wondering how they had managed to dig into the frozen ground; and then he remembered that this was New Mexico, and saw the pile of cold loose sand beside the hole. The people stood close to each other with little clouds of steam puffing from their faces. The priest looked at them and saw a pile of jackets, gloves, and scarves in the yellow, dry tumbleweeds that grew in the graveyard. He looked at the red blanket, not sure that Teofilo was so small, wondering if it wasn't some perverse Indian trick or something they did in March to ensure a good harvest, wondering if maybe old Teofilo was actually at sheep camp corralling the sheep for the night.

But there he was, facing into a cold dry wind and squinting at the last sunlight, ready to bury a red wool blanket while the faces of his parishioners were in shadow with the last warmth of the sun on their backs. His fingers were stiff, and it took him a long time to twist the the lid off the holy water. Drops of water fell on the red blanket and soaked into dark icy spots. He sprinkled the grave and the water disappeared almost before it touched the dim, cold sand; it reminded him of something, and he tried to remember what it was because he thought if he could remember he might understand this. He sprinkled more water; he shook the container until it was empty, and the water fell through the light from sundown like August rain that fell while the sun was still shining, almost evaporating before it touched the wilted squash flowers.

The wind pulled at the priest's brown Franciscan robe and swirled away the corn meal and pollen that had been sprinkled on the blanket. They lowered the bundle into the ground, and they didn't bother to untie the stiff pieces of new rope that were tied around the ends of the blanket. The sun was gone, and over on the highway the eastbound lane was full of headlights. The priest walked away slowly.

Leon watched him climb the hill, and when he had disappeared within the tall, thick walls, Leon turned to look up at the high blue mountains in the deep snow that reflected a faint red light from the west. He felt good because it was finished, and he was happy about the sprinkling of the holy water; now the old man could send them big thunderclouds for sure.

TURTLE MEAT (1983)

Joseph Bruchac III

In this strange great story about an elderly Native American who has been living for many years with a debilitated woman, Bruchac writes one of the most extraordinary fishing scenes in literature. Bruchac (born 1942) is an Abenaki poet, storyteller, and editor who lives in Greenfield Center, New York, in the Adirondack foothills.

"OLD MAN, COME in. I need you!"

The old woman's cracked voice carried out to the woodshed near the overgrown field. Once it had been planted with corn and beans, the whole two acres. But now mustard rolled heads in the wind and wild carrot bobbed among nettles and the blue flowers of thistles. *A goat would like to eat those thistles,* Homer LaWare thought. *Too bad I'm too old to keep a goat.* He put down the ax handle he had been carving, cast one quick look at the old bamboo fishing pole hanging over the door and then stood up.

"Coming over," he called out. With slow careful steps he crossed the fifty yards between his shed and the single-story house with the picture window and the gold-painted steps. He swung open the screen door and stepped over the dishes full of dog food. *Always in front of the door,* he thought.

"Where?" he called from the front room.

"Back here, I'm in the bathroom. I can't get up."

He walked as quickly as he could through the cluttered kitchen. The breakfast dishes were still on the table. He pushed open the bathroom door. Mollie was sitting on the toilet.

"Amalia Wind, what's wrong?" he said.

"My legs seem to of locked, Homer. Please just help me to get up. I've been hearing the dogs yapping for me outside the door and the poor dears couldn't even get to me. Just help me up."

He slipped his hand under her elbow and lifted her gently. He could see that the pressure of his fingers on the white wrinkled flesh of her arm was going to leave marks. She'd always been like that. She always bruised easy. But it hadn't stopped her from coming for him . . . and getting him, all those years ago. It hadn't stopped her from throwing Jake Wind out of her house and bringing Homer LaWare to her farm to be the hired man.

Her legs were unsteady for a few seconds but then she seemed to be all right. He removed his arms from her.

"Just don't know how it happened, Homer. I ain't so old as that, am I, Old Man?"

"No, Amalia. That must of was just a cramp. Nothing more than that."

They were still standing in the bathroom. Her long grey dress had fallen down to cover her legs but her underpants were still around her ankles. He felt awkward. Even after all these years, he felt awkward.

"Old Man, you just get out and do what you were doing. A woman has to have her privacy. Get now."

"You sure?"

"Sure? My Lord! If I wasn't sure you think I'd have any truck with men like you?" She poked him in the ribs. "You know what you should do, Old Man? You should go down to the pond and do that fishing you said you were going to."

He didn't want to leave her alone, but he didn't want to tell her that. And there was something in him that urged him towards that pond, the pond where the yellow perch had been biting for the last few days according to Jack Crandall. Jack had told him that when he brought his ax by to have Homer fit a new handle.

"I still got Jack's ax to fix, Amalia."

"And when did it ever take you more than a minute to fit a handle into anything, *Old Man?*" There was a wicked gleam in her eye. For a few seconds she looked forty years younger in the old man's eyes.

He shook his head.

"Miss Wind, I swear those ladies were right when they said you was going to hell." She made a playful threatening motion with her hand and he backed out the door. "But I'm going."

It took him another hour to finish carving the handle to the right size. It slid into the head like a hand going into a velvet glove. His hands shook when he started the steel wedge that would hold it tight, but it took only three strokes with the maul to put the wedge in. He looked at his hands, remembering the things they'd done. Holding the reins of the last horse they'd had on the farm—twenty years ago. Or was it thirty? Lifting the sheets back from Mollie's white body that first night. Swinging in tight fists at the face of Jake Wind the night he came back, drunk and with a loaded .45 in his hand. He'd gone down hard and Homer had emptied the shells out of the gun and broken its barrel with his maul on his anvil. Though Jake had babbled of the law that night, neither the law nor Jake ever came back to the Wind farm. It had been Amalia's all along. Her father'd owned it and Jake had married her for it. She'd never put the property in any man's name, never would. That was what she always said.

"I'm not asking, Amalia," that was what Homer had said to her after the first night they'd spent in the brass bed, just before he'd dressed and gone back to sleep the night away in his cot in the shed. He always slept there. All the years. "I'm not asking for any property, Amalia. It's the Indian in me that don't want to own no land."

That was Homer's favorite saying. Whenever there was something about him that seemed maybe different from what others expected he would say simply, "It's the Indian in me." Sometimes he thought of it not as a part of him but as another man, a man with a name he didn't know but would recognize if he heard it.

His father had said that same phrase often. His father had come down from Quebec and spoke French and, sometimes, to his first wife who had died when Homer was six, another language that Homer never heard again after her death. His father had been a quiet man who made baskets from the ash trees that grew on their farm. "But he never carried them into town," Homer said with pride. "He just stayed on the farm and let people come to him if they wanted to buy them."

The farm had gone to a younger brother who sold out and moved West. There had been two other children. None of them got a thing, except Homer, who got his father's best horse. In those years Homer was working for Seneca Smith at his mill. Woods work, two-man saws and sledding the logs out in the snow. He had done it until his thirtieth year when Amalia had

asked him to come and work her farm. Though people had talked, he had done it. When anyone asked why he let himself be run by a woman that way he said, in the same quiet voice his father had used, "It's the Indian in me."

The pond was looking glass smooth. Homer stood beside the boat. Jack Crandall had given him the key to it. He looked in the water. He saw his face, the skin lined and brown as an old map. Wattles of flesh hung below his chin like the comb of a rooster.

"Shit, you're a good-looking man, Homer LaWare," he said to his reflection. "Easy to see what a woman sees in you." He thought again of Mollie sitting in the rocker and looking out the picture window. As he left he heard her old voice calling the names of the small dogs she loved so much. *Those dogs were the only ones ever give back her love,* he thought, *not that no-good daughter. Last time she come was Christmas in '68 to give her that pissy green shawl and try to run me off again.*

Homer stepped into the boat. Ripples wiped his face from the surface of the pond. He put his pole and the can of worms in front of him and slipped the oars into the oarlocks, one at a time, breathing hard as he did so. He pulled the anchor rope into the boat and looked out across the water. A brown stick projected above the water in the middle of the pond. *Least it looks like a stick, but if it moves it . . .* The stick moved . . . slid across the surface of the water for a few feet and then disappeared. He watched with narrowed eyes until it reappeared a hundred feet further out. It was a turtle, a snapping turtle. Probably a big one.

"I see you out there, Turtle," Homer said. "Maybe you and me are going to see more of each other."

He felt in his pocket for the familiar feel of his bone-handled knife. He pushed the red handkerchief that held it deep in his pocket more firmly into place. Then he began to row. He stopped in the middle of the pond and began to fish. Within a few minutes he began to pull in the fish, yellow-stomached perch with bulging dark eyes. Most of them were a foot long. He stopped when he had a dozen and began to clean them, leaving the baited line in the water. He pulled out the bone-handled knife and opened it. The blade was thin as the handle of a spoon from thirty years of sharpening. It was like a razor. Homer always carried a sharp knife. He made a careful slit from the ventral opening of the fish up to its gills and spilled out the guts into the water, leaning over the side of the boat as he did so. He talked as he cleaned the fish.

"Old Knife, you cut good," he said. He had cleaned nearly every fish, hardly wasting a moment. Almost as fast as when he was a boy. *Some things didn't go from you so . . .*

The jerking of his pole brought him back from his thoughts. It was being dragged overboard. He dropped the knife on the seat and grabbed the pole as it went over. He pulled up on it and it bent almost double. *No fish pulls like that.* It was the turtle. He began reeling the line in, slow and steady so it wouldn't break. Soon he saw it, wagging its head back and forth, coming up from the green depths of the pond where it had been gorging on the perch guts and grabbed his worm.

"Come up and talk, Turtle," Homer said.

The turtle opened its mouth as if to say something and the hook slipped out, the pole jerking back in Homer's hands. Its jaws were too tough for the hook to stick in. But the turtle stayed there, just under the water. It was big, thirty pounds at least. It was looking for more food. Homer put another worm on the hook with trembling hands and dropped it in front of the turtle's mouth.

"Turtle, take this one too."

He could see the wrinkled skin under its throat as it turned its head. A leech of some kind was on the back of its head, another hanging onto its right leg. It was an old turtle. Its skin was rough, its shell rich with algae. It grabbed the hook with a sideways turn of its head. As Homer pulled up to snag the hook it reached forward with its paws and grabbed the line like a man grabbing a rope. Its front claws were as long as the teeth of a bear.

Homer pulled. The turtle kept the hook in its mouth and rose to the surface. It was strong and the old man wondered if he could hold it up. Did he want turtle meat that much? But he didn't cut the line. The mouth was big enough to take off a finger, but he kept pulling in line. It was next to the boat and the hook was only holding because of the pressure on the line. A little slack and it would be gone. Homer slipped the pole under his leg and grabbed with his other hand for the anchor rope, began to fasten a noose in it as the turtle shook its head, moving the twelve-foot boat as it struggled. He could smell it now. The heavy musk of the turtle was everywhere. It wasn't a good smell or a bad smell. It was only the smell of the turtle.

Now the noose was done. He hung it over the side. It was time for the hard part now, the part that was easy for him when his arms were young and his chest wasn't caved in like a broken box. He

reached down fast and grabbed the tail, pulling it so that the turtle came half out of the water. The boat almost tipped but Homer kept his balance. The turtle swung its head, mouth open and wide enough to swallow a softball. It hissed like a snake, ready to grab at anything within reach. With his other hand, gasping as he did it, feeling the turtle's rough rail tear the skin of his palm as it slipped from his other hand, Homer swung the noose around the turtle's head. Its own weight pulled the slipknot tight. The turtle's jaws clamped tight with a snap on Homer's sleeve.

"Turtle, I believe I got you and you got me," Homer said. He slipped a turn of rope around his left foot with his free arm. He kept pulling back as hard as he could to free his sleeve but the turtle had it. "I understand you, Turtle," he said, "you don't like to let go." He breathed hard, closed his eyes for a moment. Then he took the knife in his left hand. He leaned over and slid it across the turtle's neck. Dark fluid blossomed out into the water. A hissing noise came from between the clenched jaws, but the turtle held onto the old man's sleeve. For a long time the blood came out but the turtle still held on. Finally Homer took the knife and cut the end of his sleeve off, leaving it in the turtle's mouth.

He sat up straight for the first time since he had hooked the turtle and looked around. It was dark. He could hardly see the shore. He had been fighting the turtle for longer than he thought.

By the time he had reached the shore and docked the boat the sounds of the turtle banging itself against the side of the boat had stopped. He couldn't tell if blood was still flowing from its cut throat because night had turned all of the water that same color. He couldn't find the fish in the bottom of the boat. It didn't matter. The raccoons could have them. He had his knife and his pole and the turtle. He dragged it back up to the old Ford truck. It was too heavy to carry.

There were cars parked in the driveway when he pulled in. He had to park near the small mounds beside his shed that were marked with wooden plaques and neatly lettered names. He could hear voices as he walked through the darkness.

"Old fool's finally come back," he heard a voice saying. The voice was rough as a rusted hinge. It was the voice of Amalia's daughter.

He pushed through the door. "Where's Amalia?" he said. Someone screamed. The room was full of faces and they were all looking at him.

"Old bastard looks like he scalped someone," a pock-faced man with grey crew-cut hair muttered.

Homer looked at himself. His arms and hands were covered with blood of the turtle. His tattered right sleeve barely reached his elbow. His trousers were muddy. His fly was halfway open. "Where's Amalia?" he demanded again.

"What the hell have you been up to, you old fart?" said the raspy voice of the daughter. He turned to stare into her loose-featured face. She was sitting in Amalia's rocker.

"I been fishin'."

The daughter stood up and walked toward him. She looked like her father. Jake Wind was written all over her face, carved into her bones.

"You want to know where Moms is, huh? Wanta know where your old sweetheart's gone to? Well, I'll tell you. She's been sent off to a home that'll take care of her, even if she is cracked. Come in and find her sittin' talking to dogs been dead for years. Dishes full of dog food for ghosts. Maybe you better eat some of it because your meal ticket's been cancelled, you old bastard. This man is a doctor and he's decided my dear mother was mentally incompetent. The ambulance took her outta here half an hour ago."

She kept talking, saying things she had longed to say for years. Homer LaWare wasn't listening. His eyes took in the details of the room he had walked through every day for the last forty years, the furniture he had mended when it was broken, the picture window he had installed, the steps he had painted, the neatly stacked dishes he had eaten his food from three times each day for almost half a century. The daughter was still talking, talking as if this were a scene she had rehearsed for many years. But he wasn't listening. Her voice was getting louder. She was screaming. Homer hardly heard her. He closed his eyes, remembering how the turtle held onto his sleeve even after its throat was cut and its life was leaking out into the pond.

The screaming stopped. He opened his eyes and saw that the man with the grey crew-cut hair was holding the daughter's arms. She was holding a plate in her hands. Maybe she had been about to hit him with it. It didn't matter. He looked at her. He looked at the other people in the room. They seemed to be waiting for him to say something.

"I got a turtle to clean out," he said, knowing what it was in him that spoke. Then he turned and walked into the darkness.

ONLY APPROVED INDIANS CAN PLAY MADE IN USA (1983)

Jack D. Forbes

Forbes (1934–2011) was of Powhatan and Delaware heritage. Born in Long Beach, California, he earned his Ph.D. at the University of Southern California. For many years, he was a professor of Native American Studies at the University of California, Davis. "Only Approved Indians Can Play Made in USA" is almost too sad to be funny, but funny it is.

THE ALL-INDIAN BASKETBALL Tournament was in its second day. Excitement was pretty high, because a lot of the teams were very good or at least eager and hungry to win. Quite a few people had come to watch, mostly Indians. Many were relatives or friends of the players. A lot of people were betting money and tension was pretty great.

A team from the Tucson Inter-Tribal House was set to play against a group from the Great Lakes region. The Tucson players were mostly very dark young men with long black hair. A few had little goatee beards or mustaches though, and one of the Great Lakes fans had started a rumor that they were really Chicanos. This was a big issue since the Indian Sports League had a rule that all players had to be one-quarter or more Indian blood and that they had to have their BIA[2] roll numbers available if challenged.

And so a big argument started. One of the biggest, darkest Indians on the Tucson team had been singled out as a Chicano, and the crowd wanted him thrown out. The Great Lakes players, most of whom were pretty light, refused to start. They all had their BIA identification cards, encased in plastic. This proved that they

---

2. Bureau of Indian Affairs.

were all real Indians, even a blonde-haired guy. He was really only about one-sixteenth but the BIA rolls had been changed for his tribe so legally he was one-fourth. There was no question about the Great Lakes team. They were all land-based, federally recognized Indians, although living in a big Midwestern city, and they had their cards to prove it.

Anyway, the big, dark Tucson Indian turned out to be a Papago. He didn't have a BIA card but he could talk Papago, so they let him alone for the time being. Then they turned towards a lean, very Indian-looking guy who had a pretty big goatee. He seemed to have a Spanish accent, so they demanded to see his card.

Well, he didn't have one either. He said he was a full-blood Tarahumara Indian and he could also speak his language. None of the Great Lakes Indians could talk their languages so they said that was no proof of anything, that you had to have a BIA roll number.

The Tarahumara man was getting pretty angry by then. He said his father and uncle had been killed by whites in Mexico and that he did not expect to be treated with prejudice by other Indians.

But all that did no good. Someone demanded to know if he had a reservation and if his tribe was recognized. He replied that his people lived high up in the mountains and that they were still resisting the Mexicanos, that the government was trying to steal their land.

"What state do your people live in?" they wanted to know. When he said that his people lived free, outside of the control of any state, they only shook their fists at him. "You're not an official Indian. All official Indians are under the white man's rule now. We all have a number given to us, to show that we are recognized."

Well, it all came to an end when someone shouted that "Tarahumaras don't exist. They're not listed in the BIA dictionary." Another fan yelled, "He's a Mexican. He can't play. The tournament is only for Indians."

The officials of the tournament had been huddling together. One blew his whistle and an announcement was made. "The Tucson team is disqualified. One of its members is a Yaqui. One is a Tarahumara. The rest are Papagos. None of them have BIA enrollment cards. They are not Indians within the meaning of the laws of the government of the United States. The Great Lakes team is declared the winner by default."

A tremendous roar of applause swept through the stands. A white BIA official wiped the tears from his eyes and said to a companion, "God bless America. I think we've won."

HIGH COTTON (1984)

Rayna Green

Green (born in 1942) has taught at many universities and is the curator and director of the American Indian Program at the Smithsonian Institution's National Museum of American History in Washington, D.C. She earned her Ph.D. in folklore from Indiana University and edited *That's What She Said: Contemporary Poetry and Fiction by Native American Women* (1984). Green's Native background, through her father, is Cherokee.

Is EVERYTHING A story? Ramona asked her.

It is if a story's what you're looking for—otherwise, it's just people telling lies and there's no end to it. Grandma waited to see how she took that and she started in again, smoothing out the red-checked oilcloth on the kitchen table as she talked. Ramona watched the purple cockscombs she could see through the kitchen door.

You don't have to hear anything, not about the white ones or the red—nothing about any of them, and you can call 'em all lies if you want. In a way, they are all lies just like them Thunder stories Gahno tells you or like the Bible—something that happened too far back for anyone to see and too close for anyone to deny. You listen to her stories much more and you won't want to know the difference. Still, there's always choices. It's like the time Gahno was out in the cotton field—right here at the old home place, just beyond this door. We was just girls, all of us—her and me and Rose and Anna—and there was Poppa, the meanest old German bastard that ever lived. He had us out chopping cotton in the worst heat of the day. He treated Indian and white alike—you might say just like we was niggers—well, that's what Anna used to say when she had sense, but some might dispute that she ever had any at all. Anyway, a big old black snake run acrost Gahno's foot out there in the high cotton. And she commenced to screaming and run up to the house. Lord, she throwed down that hoe and hollered loud enough to make us all run up from the Field.

Snake, she hollered, snake.

But Poppa had seen the blacksnake come acrost the field and he didn't put no store at all in running from snakes. He liked to kill 'em, you know, and nail their skins up on the barn door yonder.

Goddammit, he yelled, you scheisskopf Indi'n, ain't one t'ing but one blacksnake an' he don't hurt you.

That was his way of talking when he got mad and he never could talk good English anyway. Well, we all commenced to laughing and screaming at the sight of Poppa all puffed up and Gahno scared to fits—and her no better at English than him any day. She was so damn mad she about near spit at Poppa.

Jesus no, Jesus no, he maybe not hurt me, but dat damn snake he make me hurt myself.

And then we all went to laughing like as not to stop—and she started to giggle too that way she has even now. Poppa swole up even more like a toad and marched off into the house for Momma to soothe his hurt feelings, and Gahno threw down that hoe for good. She left Tahlequah and went to Dallas and she never came back—and I follered her the next year and Rose ten years later. Poppa never forgive any of us and Gahno wasn't even his kin—but he acted like she was—so he had one heart spell too many when your Momma married her son. Betrayal was bad enough, but race mixing was worse. Marrying Indians was a damn sight worse to him. I guess he thought she'd stay and slave for him forever just like he thought we would. But he was wrong. Grandma paused for breath and then stopped, watching Ramona get up and head toward the old ice box near the sink.

I know there's another story here, Ramona said. Are you going to tell it now or should I get you more ice tea to get through it? You want me to doctor yours with some of Baby Dee's finest so you don't get hoarse?

She saw assent in Grandma's eyes so she opened the flour bin where Rose always kept the drinking whiskey—remembering Aunt Anna who always called it her heart medicine when she took it by the tablespoon ten times a day.

It's Rose I want to tell you about—and Will—and that snake wadn't just a side story. Yes, get me some of Baby Dee's good whiskey. It never hurt me nor anybody else who drank it with a clear heart. He got the trick of it from those Cherokee hill climbers you stem from, I'll say that. But your Uncle Will, he was white and he drank white whiskey. It kilt his sense and will and left nothing but feeling. Baby Dee's whiskey makes me want to go file my teeth and whip up on Andy Jackson. Just bring the jar and a bite of that ham on the sideboard, and I'll tell you the real story.

Ramona set the Mason jar of clear liquid in front of her grandmother, with the bowl of rock candy and mint leaves she favored for her particular brew. And she poured herself some into the blue enamel cup she always used when she came down home to Aunt Rose's.

To heart medicine, she said.

God knows it ain't head medicine you need, Grandma told her. You had too big a dose of that from your Daddy—thinking is the family disease.

Honey, your Uncle Will, he was just like that snake, and the Baptist Church, it was like him—they was made for one another. But he was a drinking man, and he was when Rose married him. When he couldn't get whiskey from the white bootleggers, he got it from the black ones. He never drank no Indian whiskey—not like everybody else—'cause he believed they boogered it just like Baby Dee does in truth. And that whiskey made him crazy anyway. He got worse. He didn't have nothing but the whiskey and the whiskey had him. For ten years he poured the whiskey down.

Rose got all the church women to pray and pray over him, week after week, and they kept poor Jesus awake yelling about Will's sinful state. The more they prayed and hollered over him, the more he cussed and drank. And that made them pray more. You know how them prissy Baptist women is, honey—wouldn't say shit if they had a mouthful—and they like to drove everyone to the ginmills and shake dance parlors before long. But everyone was more disgusted with Will. He'd run everybody's patience out, and if he'd been on fire, not a soul would have pissed on him to save him. He raved and carried on when Rose and Bubba took the truck from him—they hid it out in Dadayi's barn over yonder at Lost City—but he stole the tractor and drove it to the bootlegger's anyway.

Well, then one night, he put the harrow on and run that tractor over thirty acres of good lake bottom cotton, and Rose finally pitched a fit. She and Bubba tied that old drunk to the bedposts and left him there to piss and shit all over hisself and he done it— they left him for two days and more.

Thirty acres might not sound like much to you now, but it was something then. They tied him to the bed right there in that room yonder and he thrashed and cussed and rolled for three days. He threatened and begged and done damn near everything he could to get them to turn him loose. But Rose's heart had hardened— even to the point of letting her spotless house stink of drunkard's shit. On the third night, he was worse than ever before, yelling and carrying on. And Rose finally come in from the front parlor where she'd tried to sleep these nights while he was cutting up. She come in and stood at the foot of his bed.

Sister, give me just another bite of that ham and some of Gahno's bean bread before I go on. I could piece all day on that ham and never set down to a meal. There's nothing like funerals for good eating.

You better hurry with the story or they're all going to be back from the funeral parlor and hear the worst, Ramona told her. I'm going to have just a little bite myself to keep my strength up. I may need a whole ham the way you're going.

Baby Sister, I never knew you to let your strength get endangered. You're both your Grandma's child, that's for certain.

Well, Rose come into the bedroom trying to breathe in the stench and keep from laughing at the old bastard's misery at the same time. She loved seeing him as wretched as she'd been all these years. So she stood at the foot of the bed, all dressed in an old white flannel gown—the same old one she'd worn for ten years and the one she would wear today if they hadn't bought that silly blue town dress just to go to the boneyard. So there she stood in that ruffled white flannel gown, and Will, crazy with having the whiskey took from him, thought it was Jesus come to take him away. He seen the ghosts and boogers of his worst drunk dreams and commenced to bleat and call out to Jesus. Guilty through all the whiskey boldness, he called out to Jesus and begged Him not to take him now.

Jesus, I been bad I know, but I'll be good tomorrow. Jesus, I'm not ready now, but give me another chance to serve you. Jesus, I'll praise your name tomorrow and never take another drop of drink.

Well, sir, he went on like that 'til Rose got tickled and you know what a cut-up she is when she gets provoked. So, she started to laugh for all those ten years of suffering with that drunken worthless farmer, and she begin to shake that white gown and talk to him. So, she made out to him like she was Jesus. Well, if he could give up his sins, she reasoned, why couldn't she take some up since there'd be room left in the emptiness.

Oh, Will, she said, talking deep, I've got plans for you. I need a sober man, a righteous man, a just man. I've got plans for your life, but you'll have to promise me to quit drinking and whoring and treating your good wife so bad.

Oh, Jesus, I will, I will do it, he yelled. Jesus, I'm the one to do it.

Will, she said, waving her arms and standing on tiptoe in the kerosene light—her gown all cloudy and white around her—I want you to come out of that piss and shit, out of the hog wallow you've fallen in, and I want you to preach my word.

Oh, Jesus, he promised, I'm the one.

Well, she damn near kilt herself laughing, but she went on until they was both worn out with it and he promised to preach Jesus' word until he died. When she'd calmed herself, Will was still a-raving about Jesus. But she looked at that piece of stinking flesh on the bed and thought about murder. She picked up the jonny pot from under the bed and tried to break his head with it. She picked up the pissy sheets and tried to strangle him around his turkey neck, and she offered to smother him with the last of her good feather pillows.

But Jesus had him no matter what she done, and he lived and praised her, thinking all the time it was Jesus putting him to the test. And well it might have been. But wanting to kill him so bad and Jesus saving him made her hate the church on the spot. She thought if he did wake up and fulfill his promise to preach, it was a church she didn't want nothing to do with it anyway. Well, the Devil didn't offer her a solution and the little son-of-a-bitch didn't die. So, she took off that white gown and threw it into the bed with him.

It ain't Jesus, you damned old fool, she up and screamed at him, it's your crazy wife and be damned to the both of you.

She boiled up water for the hottest bath she'd ever had and sat buck naked at the parlor pump organ all night, playing every shake dance tune she knew, and she was sitting there when Baby Dee come to start plowing in the morning. She was laughing and singing and happy like he's never seen her, and he couldn't believe his ears when she asked him if he'd ever thought of taking his whiskey-making skills to Dallas. They was gone before Will come to, and when he did, he took her leaving for the punishment he deserved. He cleaned himself up and went right uptown to the preacher to confess his sins and sign up for the Jesus Road.

Rose and Baby Dee went right to Dallas with Gahno and the other Indians that had left before, and that's where we all ended up—that is, until Will died fifteen years ago as sober as when he was born. But she'd had the good time and he'd paid for what he done to her by living a strict and righteous life. She'd takened away the only thing he loved, and ended up making her living selling it.

And Jesus done it all, she would tell people.

There's a white flannel salvation that comes to drunks in the dark and makes 'em change. So she wondered when it would come to her. She got Baby Dee to booger his whiskey too, so wouldn't nobody get saved on it and tot up more souls for Jesus. She used to tell him—we're in the whiskey business, not the salvation business. Jesus looked like an Arab and dressed like a woman and that ain't what we're about. And they'd go on up to the stomp dances in the hills after they'd come back here to live, never drinking one drop of the whiskey they made, 'cause she'd turned Indian just as sure as she'd turned away from Christians, and that would have driven a nail into Poppa's heart too. She always figured, just like Gahno, that snakes was meant to warn you, and she took the warning.

Well, that's the story and there's no end to it. There's more than one thing that will make you hurt yourself and more than one that'll save you.

Jesus, Ramona said.

Yes, Jesus, Grandma said.

There's the picture of Poppa and Will on the wall, where they belong—in stockmen's suits and French silk kerchiefs. And here's the rest of us—you and Momma and Baby Dee and Gahno and me—gone to the Indians or to Dallas or to some of those strange places you favor. Except for Rose, who's laying dead up town. At least we won't have no one preach over her. She can take that comfort. We can just sing and tell lies when they all come back to the house, and the Indians can bury her the right way tomorrow. You and Baby Dee can do it right. Maybe Baby Dee will take a drink of his own whiskey today.

More stories? Ramona asked.

Snakebite medicine, Grandma said.

SNATCHED AWAY (1988)

Mary TallMountain

Athabascan, Koyukon, and Russian on her mother's side, Mary TallMountain was born Mary Demoski in northern Alaska in 1918. She lived for many years in San Francisco and died in 1994.

NEAR FOUR MILE summer camp, the Indians were nudging their fishwheel into calmer water. The Yukon was in a fierce, frowning mood. It tossed spray hissing skyward, hurled it back down like heavy rain into the weltering currents. Where stubborn little creeks shouldered out insistently, the river surged to attack, writhing up in silt-brown rapids. Accustomed to its tempers, the men kept tending the wheel, which alternately plunged two carved spruce arms into the current to rotate with the tide. An oblong wire basket at the end of the arm scooped up fish; on the next rotation, as the arm tipped, the fish slithered into a box nailed to the raft deck of the fishwheel; the arm loomed up again like a windmill blade, fell back, and turned with the force of the tides. The ascent of dog salmon heralded the coming of autumn; fish flowed in a stream of silvery rose.

Quick dark silhouettes against the greens of alder and cottonwood, the Indians were part of sky, river, earth itself: they wove dories through tumbling water, poled schools of darting salmon, strode like lumberjacks. Born rivermen, Clem thought with respect. Still, the river was a tough customer. In the seven years he'd been here, ten men and boys had drowned between Nulato and Kaltag.

Andy was the latest, and him only twenty-two.

The day in 1916 when Clem had unloaded his gear at Nulato
Garrison, he had met fifteen-year-old Andy on the riverbank,
where the Army had barged the new soldiers upriver. A crooked
tooth leaning into his wide white grin, the lad had offered to help
Clem with his violin and banjo cases. Even then, Andy was the
best there was: hunter, fisherman, trapper, nobody could beat him.
Only the river could have beaten Andy.

Clem's boat chugged into the immense, misted expanses.

He wondered how Andy had felt, knowing himself caught,
fighting. Did he see sky and trees flashing past? How long had he
struggled, tumbled over and over in the fast rips out here where
nothing existed to snag a man and hold him solid so he could keep
his head above the deadly tides? Andy had never been found,
though two months had passed. A cry had been heard on shore,
but when the men got out and rowed toward the sound, only the
voice of the river met them. Andy's empty canoe had floated in a
gentle riff behind the island of silt growing in mid-stream.

Their friendship had stretched through the years. Clem had
eaten with Andy's large family, gone with the men on hunting
trips when he had leave from duty. He had thought the natives
liked him as well as any *Gisakk*, the word they had for white men.

Clem thought of the afternoon he had spent talking on the riverbank with Andy and Little Jim. He thought Little Jim was related
too, some way. Cousins, maybe? He couldn't find out how these
people were hooked up together. Something about the families,
how their forebears were related, the kinship among the whole
Athabascan people, was dim and old as time.

*Clem glanced over at Andy now and then. He had already discovered that
these natives didn't like to be stared at; he tried to keep them from catching
him. Andy didn't seem to notice. In the tall grass he lounged on his side,
wearing a white man's wool shirt and store-bought overalls, chewing a grass
stem, fur cap low over his eyes. He looked just like his father, Big Mike,
the stubby Russian, the way Mike must have looked when he was fifteen
and a lot skinnier. Andy's eyes were fixed on the river. About fifty feet
out, a small bundle came rolling down fast, something tied tight in a
gunnysack.*

"Hey what's that?" Clem asked.

"Yeah," Little Jim muttered.

*"It's a baby," Andy said, following it with his gaze as it tossed and
turned round and round downriver.*

"What the hell?" Clem thought he'd heard wrong.

"Baby. Throwed away." Andy chewed fast, wagging the grass back and forth. "When baby come out, maybe he got bum leg, maybe no leg, or he come out wrong, head mashed. Women say he's no good, tie him up, dump him over riverbank." He appeared to draw in his breath, but Clem couldn't fathom any change in his expression. "They use to do it in old time," Andy said. "Things were worse then. They quit doing it, but sometimes women still throw them if they're too bad." Andy looked out over the river, barely rippling, shining, innocent. A flock of snowgeese, in formation passing south, announced their departure in ancient ceremonial voice.

Little Jim said, "Lots of babies die in old time. They get Gisakk disease. That mean white-man sickness. We got a doctor now, but when Grandfather was living it was real bad. The people name him Old Russian."

Clem asked, "How did Old Russian get here on the river?"

Andy said, "Grandfather—well, he's really my grandfather's papa, you know, he come upriver with three Russians. We call them Gisakk too, like all white men. They talk-talk all the time, maybe we call them that name because they talk about Cossack, it go round, get to be called Gisakk." Both men chuckled as if at an old joke. Andy went on, "But then came other Russians, buy furs from our people in our old hunting mountains, we call Kaiyuh. Those ones build big Russian kashim to live in, and traders post store, on the river south of where Nulato sits now." He pointed the grass stem south. "Down there. That town is all gone now. Koyukuk warrior start war, burn down kashim, everybody die inside." Silence followed while the men considered the ancient violence.

"After they die, sickness come," Little Jim said. "First, it's smallpox. Old people say Gisakk bring it, who knows where it come from. No way to write it down. That's long time ago. Those people only talk, not read. Now we have this new sickness, this consumption, TB."

"That pretty bad?" Clem asked.

Little Jim frowned. "Yeah, no way to cure that when it get ahold. If they could go Outside, there's hospitals for it, but who could go Outside? Cost too much dinga." He rubbed his thumb against his finger in the universal sign for money.

Andy swept his arm wide. "Many other ways to die, though," he said, crossing his legs, settling deeper into the grass. "Sometimes a house catch fire, we fight it with river water, maybe people burn up anyway. Short life for some of us. That's why our people get married so young." He laughed.

Little Jim stared downriver. "Lots of people drown. The current play tricks, hide, next thing it's got you. Pretty near got me, couple times." He grinned. *"We don't swim. Nobody swims."*

"Jesus," Clem said.

With a heave of brown water, the river slammed a log into the bow of the boat, jolting Clem out of his flashes of reverie. Whew! No damage done! Seven years ago, he would have been alert to the river's tricks at a safe enough distance to get out of the way, he thought, steering away from the middle. The river hadn't been too tough for him back then; he was already a rugged fellow fresh from cavalry duty on the Mexican border, lean as a malamute, hair a sunbleached shock against perennially brown skin. His intent sea-colored eyes incessantly changed with the lights, focusing as if to X-ray everything he saw. His air was alert and confident. Seven years on the Yukon had converted him into a critter tough as walrus hide. It was his first taste of the wilderness: raising dogs, training them for sled work and distance travel; running search-rescue missions by dogteam in winter, by motorboat in summer. All around him stretched the stark and beautiful land. He tried to write his feelings in notes of music on scraps like the secret fragments of a poet, but they escaped him.

Away in a corner of his mind, an old piano tinkled, playing Mary Joe's favorites, "Yum Yum Waltz" and "Pitti Sing Polka." The notes echoed tinnily in his head. At Ruby, a red-hot boom town, he had been playing the tunes steadily for the past three days and nights. The miners and whores had hollered for dance music. He had rounded up young Charlie Wilson, a native banjo picker, and they went up by motorboat. Those wild rough folks had insisted on high jinks and kept Clem and Charlie playing day and night. Wouldn't let them rest, threw gold and dollar bills to them, yelled for them to keep going, offered bad bootleg he and Charlie waved away. The boys worked themselves so dizzy that Charlie had stayed on with kinfolks for a visit. Clem was dog-tired, he was homesick, he'd been away from Mary Joe too long already.

His biceps were numb from the kick of the tiller against him; that fast leaping current was deadly; he kept veering into it. Twenty- and thirty-foot trees tumbled up like matchsticks, roots clawing toward the sky. He swung over, pivoted the boat into still water. Even after he dropped anchor, the river kept grabbing, trying to yank him back. He knuckled his eyes. When his vision cleared, he saw tall green reeds in a slough sixty yards off. Suddenly a clump of ducks rose, bunched, started climbing. Shots cracked. Clem flattened fast. Four birds dropped; the flock fluttered south out of gunsight.

Who the hell is it? I didn't see a boat, he thought. Nothing moved. Then Floyd Tommy pried out of the reeds, holding a bunch of mallards. He ambled over. "Got a couple." He held up the birds. "I come down here early, before the sun. Sometimes a few duck stop here."

"Nice fat mallard," Clem said.

"Not so bad, been feedin' all summer." Floyd's gangling young body was wet to his waist.

"Scared them up, I guess," Clem said, climbing out of the boat, his red rubber Pacs plopping in the water. Ice tingled clear through the heavy rubber, the thick wool socks, on up the long johns.

"Feeding off of the bottom," Floyd said and grabbed a duck by its ringed neck, and a second. He dropped them on the grass. "Grub for the pot, anyways."

"That's swell. Thanks." Clem admired the birds, the green shine of their feathers.

"Nothing extra," Floyd said.

Clem fished out a tin of King Albert. "Take a smoke," he offered.

Floyd pocketed the tobacco. He coughed deeply and spit. The spit hung on a weed, a strand of pink swaying in the wind. He walked away and Clem saw his sharp shoulderblades, thin butt. Consumption, he thought. Kid shouldn't smoke. Sorry I gave him tobacco.

Clem crawled up the bank, lay flat under a tree. Fine here, let his whole body go quiet, he thought, let the stillness float into and around him while he stared at the scrambled pale sky.

Kid's cough made him think of Mary Joe.

Right after Clem had come to Nulato, he'd struck up an acquaintance with Cap Jaeger, the trader. They played fiddle and guitar for dances, with Freddy Kriska jingling and clinking away on his banjo. They practiced in Cap's store.

One evening Clem went outside to take a breath. Mary Joe was sitting on the porch step. He couldn't resist. He laid his hand on her gleaming, waist-long hair, bound with a bright purple band. "What a beautiful girl," he said. Once he'd seen her running through the village, hair flying, had seen that even in shapeless trousers and faded cotton shirt, she was lovely.

She got up; her smile seemed to glow in the dusk as she floated closer in a movement sensuous as a cat's; they faced each other. He smelled wind and furs, and something elusive like sweet grass.

They stood motionless, barely breathing. Then she broke the hush. "I'm about as tall as you, Clem Stone. You're my brother's friend. You know, Andy. I come and listen to you play music, but I always go away. This time, I risk it."

"That's no risk, girl. I'm not dangerous," he murmured. The very air felt electric with the closeness of her.

"Oh, yes, you are," she said. She pulled out a large white handkerchief, coughed lightly into it. A tingling—was it a foreshadowing of an unknowable sorrow?—shivered along his nerves. Somehow, he sensed, it broke an impasse.

She told him she'd just turned twenty-one. She lived with her father, her brother Andy, and a younger brother, Steven. Her mother, Matmiya, two sisters, and a third brother had died of TB. Times were bad for the people. She did laundry for soldiers at the station. They wore "Alaska Warmies," a special Army issue of long johns, and the damned brown Army soap shrank them midget-sized. Mary Joe had a special way to wash them. It kept her busy, along with looking after her menfolk, getting in a little fishing, tending a few traps.

Just surviving, she had skills he'd never known existed. The traps and snares she so carefully laid, empty when the animals couldn't come out to tackle the howling cold. Wolves running hungry. Moose, caribou, galloping broomstick thin before the wolves.

And in the village, the hungry children.

Affection for her family was part of the whole business of hunger, he thought. It hadn't been like that with his folks, back in California. Hardly a time he could remember when Pa or even Ma showed their love for him and brother Jass, except when they were tykes, and then it was like he dreamed it. Becky, his mother, was always wrapped in thought, eyes far away, lips moving. How badly he wanted to get into her head! She kept her thoughts wrapped up inside, the way she wrapped her outside, in dark dresses and big white aprons with tails that tied round and round and hid her tiny waist. He hoped she was happy at last. She'd finally married Balch Jopson, the hired man, after she divorced Pa. Right away, Pa married that woman from Hoptown. Pure orneriness. Pa had that terrible temper . . . suspicioned Balch and Becky so hard he finally had to leave her. Clem frowned. He'd never figured out why as a kid he'd been jealous over Becky and Balch too . . . Vaguely, he knew he'd inherited a trait of jealousy. He supposed he'd got it from Pa. When he thought of Mary Joe and Taria, he got too mad to talk. She had married that old man when she was fourteen, had a son the next year. Not long ago, Taria had gone down to live in Kaltag and had taken their son with him. Why had she let that boy go, and him only five? When Clem tried to talk to her about it, she always got him off the track with a funny remark or dinner on the table, or lovemaking, anything to derail him.

Mary Joe was jealous too, in her secret way. There was the day he'd been talking to young Talla and Mary Joe came along the boardwalk, stalked right up to them, and walloped him a good one on the jaw. She never mentioned it afterwards, but it kind of lay there between them. Mary Joe had wanted one of those little medicine sacks made of caribou hide, to hang on her belt. He'd asked Talla to make one, and he'd been telling her how the initials ought to be. Mary Joe thought he was sparking the girl! Well, jealousy or no, Clem and Mary Joe had given Lidwynne and Michael enough love to last a lifetime.

His mind magnetized to a worry that had been shoved back, these few hectic days. He and Mary Joe were about to lose their kids. She had found out from Doc Merrick that she had consumption, and he had offered to adopt them. Mary Joe had got so worked up over that, he realized, she'd forgotten Clem's last hitch was about up. Strange, but no use worrying yet. He'd just have to let things take their course. Hell, like he always figured, it would come out in the wash. . . .

A jay screamed from a lodge-pole pine. Clem stood, whirled his arms, kneaded his shoulders, took a fast run along the beach and back. New energy shuttled through his blood. Kicking the boat off, he noticed his tiller arm had eased up. He'd make it. He had a damn good bulge of strength in those biceps. But his calculation had misfired again. As usual, he had underrated the river. The damned thing yanked him every which way. Time blurred. No-Oy, as the natives called the sun, was well up the sky. Its light dazzled him and he centered in again on the tiller. God! that sprint of energy hadn't lasted! At last, through his daze, he saw Pete Slough alongside. Soft grayblue wings of a pair of teal flapped, rose. His eyes swarmed with blurs as he turned from the river glare, staggered stiffly up the bank.

Willy Pitka was netting whitefish in the ruffled water of the slough. He hauled in three fish, ten to fourteen inches long, threw them into a washtub. Willy looked as if he had always been there. He was strong, fierce-looking like most of the Ten'a Athabascans; good hunter, ten kids working every day, well fed. "Fishing pretty good today," Willy said, pointing to the nearly filled tub.

Clem pummeled his cramp-knotted arm, "Good big fish," he said.

"You come down from Ruby, yah?" Willy eased the handwoven net into the water. It flowed between his chunky fingers, barely rippling into the water.

"Been playing for a dance up there," Clem said, walking back and forth, the numbness inching out of his knees.

"River pretty fast, plenty wood coming down," Willy said.

"It was real bad a few miles. Got tired fighting it and stopped up yonder, below Tommy's camp. Floyd was getting a few mallard."

Willy nodded. "There's a few places up there, duck come every year about this time. Floyd knows them pretty good. Oh, yeah, you got to watch that river."

"Need eyes in back of your head. Easier in winter when she's frozen over," Clem said.

"You still got your lead dog, Beauty?" Willy asked.

"You bet. She's my brood mother, pure malamute. I've got the best team on the river. Hey, you know Manuska built me a dogsled all spruce, not a nail, bound with walrus hide. Laid it around the joints wet, and it dried like iron."

"How much you pay him?"

"Couple sawbucks."

"Worth it. You take care of your team there at the station?"

"Yeah. Got a pot outside to boil their fish. I got three males, two females, out of Beauty. Bought my breeder, Moose, from old man Patsy, set me back fifty but he's worth every cent. Saved my bacon more'n once on the trail. He knows everything, even in the worst storms."

Willy chuckled. "Like you got money in the bank. Uncle Sam has to pay every time you use that team for Army business, yah?"

"Paid for itself a hundred times over." Clem pulled out a package of salmon strip and biscuit. The rich smoke made his taste buds water. He lay back and eased his shoulder muscles into the sun-warm padding of dry reeds. He looked up at the willows. They leaned nearly horizontal over the water. Fallen trees had been bleached to ivory skeletons, and lay crushed and scattered. Small waves slapped the sides of Willy's dory. The watery sounds soothed Clem to sleep.

"You got it made better'n three-quarters downriver to home now." The voice was just loud enough. Guess Willy figured I'd snooze too long, Clem thought. Time to get on. The voice continued, "You going to Nulato?" Willy's dense eyebrows almost grazed his straight soot-colored lashes.

"That's where I'm heading. Two, maybe three hours?"

"Three hours do it, I guess," Willy said, hauling net. He tossed another pair of whitefish into the tub, piled the net with great care into the dory. His teeth gleamed with good humor.

"Your camp downriver a ways?" Clem asked. He stretched and yawned. He thought, I'm rested now, maybe I can make it before dark.

"Yeah, we use the same old camp. Had that camp many years. Good run on kings this summer. Usually I come up here, get whitefish, let my boys handle the wheel."

Clem looked south. Away, faint in the clear air, the purple crest of the Kaiyuh range rested on the horizon. "Willy!" He pointed. "You think there's a Woodsman in Kaiyuh?"

Willy's face crinkled around the grin in tiny rolls of brown, velvety skin. "Oh, sure. Lotsa Woodsman over there."

"You ever see one?" Clem wasn't sure Willy was on the level. Probably joshing him.

"Yep. Mad like bear, bad like bear. Steal babies." Willy's crinkles deepened and formed fans. They laughed.

"So long, Willy."

"See you."

Clem stepped into his boat and pulled the starter cord. The engine barked and on the next yank snapped to life. Almost at once, the boat kept trying to get out of his hands and pull out into the heavy rip. He needed all his wits just keeping her steady outside the churning middle river. A red horde of dog salmon thrashed upriver. They leaped against the edges of the riptide, fell back. He steered away, the tiller held hard against his body. It's a stampede out there, he thought, looking over his shoulder at the line of furious red dog salmon action. There's something besides fish alive, out in that river.

He had a sudden sense of repeated time, of some old and half forgotten grief.

He was carrying Lidwynne along a village path, and her frosty breaths puffed out on the windless air. Mary Joe's boots padded behind him as his heavy steps angrily crunched the snow. He held the swinging lantern; its light bobbed in yellow winkings. His mind babbled. We will go on through the night snow and we will never come back. We will go to the hills, Mary Joe. They will never part us. She caught up with him. There was no sound as Mary Joe looked into the baby's face. The moon reflected roundly silver in her pupils. Snow drifted down out of the spruces. The silence was broken by a sighing sound, descending from an immense distance. His anger left him. Only weariness remained. He turned with Mary Joe and they went back. Inside the cabin, he laid the baby in bed and kissed the corner of her sleeping mouth.

At his shoulder, Mary Joe said, "You can't have her. She must go somewhere else." His breath was heavy; he heard the muffled beating of his heart. Her face was deep in the shadows. "Clem, I have a new baby in here." She laid his hand on her belly and they rested on the lynx-fur blankets. His mind played a small wandering melody; they drifted to sleep.

He did not know whether it was a dream or a strange, obscure knowledge; now it had come again to him in the fury of the river, the somber weariness of his body; he saw their faces in the aimless, enclosing mists of the Yukon, and he knew it would be so for all of his life.

He looked at his hands, rigidly white on the tiller. Needles of ice prodded them. The beaver-lined moosehide mittens he had forgotten to bring flashed into his mind. Mary Joe had sewn and beaded them.

Her face came toward him. The high flush of her flaring cheekbones. The gentle hollows beneath. The eyes he could never describe. The children, their laughter flashing white. Three faces together, wavering in the thin and growing mist.

Indian. Indianness. The words floated through his thoughts. He jerked his head, trying to flick away the daze. He shouted into the mist, "What difference now, how much the blood is mixed? Our kids are as much Irish or Russian or Scotch as Indian. What difference now?"

His words were snatched away by the wind.

CROW'S SUN (1991)

Duane Niatum

Duane Niatum was born in 1938 and has lived most of his life in Seattle, Washington. His poems, stories, and essays have appeared in over one hundred magazines and newspapers in the United States and Europe. He has taught grade school, high school, and at several universities in the U.S., most recently at Western Washington University. He has received international acclaim for his poems and stories, has been translated into fourteen languages, and is the recipient of numerous literary awards. He was nominated four times for the Pushcart Prize. He was invited to read at the International Poetry Festival in Rotterdam, the Netherlands, and The Library of Congress. He is an enrolled member of the Klallam Tribe (Jamestown Band). He has a Ph.D. in American Studies from the University of Michigan/Ann Arbor.

Service by Native Americans in the U.S. Armed Forces has a long and complicated history. "Crow's Sun," one episode of that history, is about a young soldier sentenced to the brig.

ALL MORNING THOMAS has tied himself into a rug of knots over the verdict. Since yesterday he has known that he was sentenced to spend time in the brig. The usual bureaucratic red tape has prolonged his transfer until after lunch, much of which he cannot even look at, much less eat.

From Keyport the ride in the jeep into the Naval Shipyard at Bremerton is completely silent. While still at the mess hall he caught wind of the rumor circulating at the table across from him that his punishment has already started. Since they pulled out of the main gate, the Shore Patrolman has not looked at him or said a word. He thinks his uneasiness is more a result of Raven's tricks than any act of the SP. The day is the warmest and brightest it has been all spring. As he walked to the jeep he inhaled several deep breaths of air that told him summer would be a very special event. The miles and miles of silence make him feel like they have been driving through a narrow tunnel. It adds to the way the air now suffocates. Thus the challenge awaiting him at the end of this road forms like spiked clouds on a long flight through a storm. In the Navy a year now, he still cannot fathom why sailors 17 to 70 live in some dream of future glory which is the oldest myth of the military. It is the one thing they use to measure their lives and all the meaning they want from their lives. At least this is what every man on the base has shown him in the last year. Each man looks, talks and acts like everyone else on the base. The image that first came to mind was an army of drone ants marching into the corner. He shuddered when this happened. To him, this prison is far worse than thirty days in the marine brig.

The Navy SP swerves the jeep into one of the designated parking areas, outside the Marine Brig, and orders Thomas to get out. They step briskly as they reach the door. While waiting for someone to answer the bell, Cook, the SP, forces a smile, and speaks.

"This hole'll be your home for thirty days, Thomas. And buddy, you'd better watch your mouth in this joint. Do your time with your trap shut, until you're running free. Don't act the wise-guy. I don't like your face, Thomas, but I don't think those hicks from the base were right. You're a punk, but who isn't at your age? They went too far. I believe burning a man at the stake's too much like what I left in Alabama."

Thomas wonders why Cook bothers to tell him this. Since they first met they have never liked one another. Cook, a career man with four hashmarks, is a spit and polish sailor married to the idea that blind obedience to orders is the only law. Thomas realized almost immediately after his enlistment that he had made a mistake when he had let his parents talk him into joining up. Because he was under-age, they both had to sign papers before the Navy would accept him. Very confused about what to do with himself at his age, he let his mother and step-father talk him into enlisting. His step-father and mother had already ordered him to move out of the house, when he had stopped his step-father from beating up his mother in a drunken brawl. When he had thrown his step-father to the ground and held him down that way after saying he better not ever try hitting him again if he wanted to stay in one piece, he knew his life was headed in another direction.

"You're not exactly what I would call a friend, Cook, but you've never proven an enemy either. So what's your news?"

"Well, a few of the guys you tangled with on the base called the brig warden and painted an ugly picture of you. I know for a fact that they told the brig warden he ought to break both your legs. If you got any sense in that thick skull of yours, you'll be careful. With eyes in the back of your head."

"Thanks for the tip, Cook. It's good to see you haven't given everything to that tin badge and 45. I may be Indian at heart, but I can appreciate a brother with a tiny bit of soul."

Cook laughs and the tension evaporates like water in July.

"Sure, arrowhead, black's beautiful—all that jazz—but remember, you better be on your toes with these marines. They don't play and most are mad-dogs from hell. Being a high-yellow redskin isn't going to help your ass in the brig. It could even add to the danger. You understand what I'm telling you? Don't be a goddamn hot-head!"

Thomas assures him that he knows what they are like in the brig. He has heard a few men tell their own stories of the situation. After a grunt or two, a marine private opens the huge steel door, and the two men enter. Everything glistens in the dim light like an anesthetized tomb. In a room at the end of the brassy corridor, a man with a handlebar mustache sits at a desk. He looks to be checking a record or report and ignores or does not hear the men approach. Cook motions Thomas to stand at attention inside the door as he walks up to talk with the sergeant at the desk: the Brig Warden.

"Got another one for you, Sergeant. Name's Young Thomas." The Sergeant glances at Thomas a moment, without looking at Cook.

"Yes, we've been expecting him, bosun. You can head back to the base; we'll take care of him real good for you. Don't worry about a thing."

"Right, Sergeant." Cook turns smartly. In passing Thomas, he slaps Thomas's arm lightly with his club, and goes out the door. With a quick nod, Thomas acknowledges Cook's way of saying good luck, but he can't help wondering if a Black Panther or a Muslim will ever challenge the older man before the State cancels him in retirement. He shrugs his shoulders when he remembers he has never believed in miracles or gods.

The sergeant glares indifferently at Thomas for several minutes and then returns to the papers on his desk. He grasps a pencil and rolls it back and forth rhythmically between his hands, ignoring the stranger standing like a statue at the door. The sounds Thomas hears are the sergeant's slow breathing and the pencil striking the different bulky rings on his fingers. From the corner of his eye, Thomas notices the other man swing back in his chair and look directly into his eyes. Thomas almost flinches. Realizing it is the first time the Sergeant has said a word to him, he breathes more evenly.

"You see that yellow line in front of my desk, boy?" The younger man looks down at the yellow line that the Sergeant is pointing at. "Well, get your ass in front of that line, boy. When I look down again, I sure as hell better not see your shoes touching it. Now move!"

Looking triumphant, the Sergeant bends forward, flings his pencil on the desk, and begins thumbing through the papers stacked in front of him. He mutters about the fucking rat race he has chosen for himself and how many years he has to count like little sticks of memory before he can retire to his home in Mississippi across that magic Mason-Dixon Line. He mumbles on of the endless duplication of junk and faces, the routine eating away at him like lice. How he would prefer to be any place in the world rather than in this hole.

Still standing at attention inside the pit, before the Sergeant's desk and yellow line, Thomas looks straight ahead. His friends have warned him of the prison; the men who run it. He focuses his eyes on a notice tacked to the wall behind the Sergeant's desk. It reads in bold-face type:

A Marine has no friends.
A Marine wants no friends.

Casually, as if just waking up, the Sergeant lets his eyes drift down to Thomas's shoes and the yellow line.

"What's your name, boy?"

"Young Thomas."

The Sergeant's jaws flush; grow puffy. He lurches from his chair almost knocking it over. The muscles in Thomas's face tighten; his eyes thicken; narrow into tiny moons peering from behind a shield of fern. He sways slightly; stiffens his whole body, not sure what to expect from the man closing in. Grandson to Cedar Crow, Thomas feels his fingers change to claws, to a wing of thrashing spirit flying wildly inside his ear. (Be calm and steady now. This man could be your enemy. Know his every move. Break him like a twig if he tries to harm you. Be the Thunderbird of our song. I am Crow, your father.)

Suddenly, the Sergeant's short grunts of breath beat his face. Thomas searches for the owl spirit in the eye of the man looming toward him; they are gray and crystalline. Death is not flying in those crystals. He relaxes as the blood returns from his eyes to his feet; watches the Sergeant's mustache twitch around pock-marks. Words spit into his face, yet the cell remains whole. Owl has not chosen this life.

"What did you say, boy?"

"I said, Young Thomas, Sergeant."

Nearly uncaged now, the Sergeant pants in a faster rhythm. His well-creased shirt is saturated with large sweat-patches, the wrinkles spread down his chest and arms. He grabs the younger man by the neck, drags him to the wall. Thomas does not resist. A river bird builds a nest at the center of the storm in his heart; his thoughts run for the longhouse of Old Tillicum at Salmon Bay Village.

Mechanically, the Sergeant slams Thomas's head against the wall; kicks his shoes together. Reluctantly, he releases the young man's neck. He shoves him as he steps back. He straightens his tie and wipes his brow to regain his composure; authority.

"Listen, punk. And listen hard. Down here, morning, noon or night, when a marine asks you to open that idiotic mouth of yours, you remember to say, sir. Sir! SIR! And you little bastard, you'd better not forget it!"

Carried away by this impulse, the Sergeant grabs Thomas's head and slams it against the wall again. Apparently satisfied, he returns to his desk and hollers.

"Did you get that, boy?"

"Yes, sir."

Thomas hears his most pessimistic teachers and friends claim there is nothing but ashes in the forests of the Klallam people. Or nothing of value. Since his grandfather, his first teacher and friend, had dropped among the cedars and pines to become another dead root, he had nearly succumbed to this belief himself, he heard it so much all during his childhood. Although his grandfather, the guardian of his zig-zag path, had died a year earlier, the quiet man of family, sea and forest had counseled him well. Young was convinced it was his grandfather who made the sunrise and sunset real and at anchor in his heart. Because of this man the seasons would show some promise. Although the ancestral longhouse and fishing village was destroyed long ago by hordes of white settlers streaming into every inch of the land of the Seven Brothers, he had made a covenant in blood to the old ones in his family to wear his grandfather's feather and path to the grave.

"Yes, sir."

"Now, get your ass in front of that line."

The Sergeant leans back in his chair, leaving two hand prints on the glass desktop. The chair squeaks.

"Who the hell are you, boy? What'd you say your name was?"

"Young Thomas, sir!"

"That's more like it. How old are you, boy?"

"Eighteen, sir."

"Just a goddamn punk, aren't ya'?"

(Keep close to the winter fire and winter songs, your family circle; join in the sing, little Crow. Hear the drum and your family songs lessen the weight of the dark.)

"Yes, sir."

"Let me hear you say, 'I'm a fucking idiot, sir.'"

(Little crow, life'll feel a waste sometime, a flood of wrong paths, an earthquake of mistakes. When this happens, grandson, seek the friendship of your elder brother Courage. Listen for his song. Stay alert for when grandmother red cedar becomes a branch of your shadow. It's like dying, little crow. It's like being reborn too. So it was with my grandfather's life, so it'll be with your life and your son's son. Pain's the father of life but the river's your mother and night your chosen guardian. Listen to their stories show the way out of the storm.)

"You're a . . . I mean, I'm a fucking idiot, sir!"

The sergeant smiles and chuckles to himself. He takes a handkerchief from his pocket and systematically wipes his forehead and hands, and then continues.

"Know just what you are, don't ya', boy?"

"Yes, sir."

"Say, mush face, a few swab-jocks from Keyport been tellin' me you're a real wise guy. Read a lot of Commie shit. Think you're some kind of revolutionary. Are you a troublemaker, boy?"

"No, sir."

"Everybody from Keyport been telling me a different story, boy. They tell me you're a tough guy. You look more like a bag of bones to me. Ha! Yes, sir, more like a coon man slipping down a magnolia tree. Ha! Ha! Well, can you dig a hole like a pig, boy?"

"No, sir."

"Christ, boy, can't you howl like a cat?"

"I guess so, sir."

"I guess so, sir. You fucking idiot! Don't ya' know nothing?"

"I guess not, sir."

"All right, stupid. What's your serial number?"

"995 57 15, sir."

"Where were you born, punk?"

"Seattle, Washington, sir."

Slow and methodical, the Sergeant inches his way around the desk to stand in front of Thomas. He plans to bury the next questions in the younger man's soul.

"Who ya' trying to kid with a name like Thomas, boy? How's a wetback like you got a name like Thomas? Ain't it really Pancho Villa or Willy Garcia? Ha!"

"I'm not from Mexico, sir. I . . ."

"In my book you're a fucking wetback. Shit you're a wetback from head to toe. Who you kidding, boy?"

Thomas stares back into the two gray crystals. He watches the sweat roll down the Sergeant's temples. He feels it roll down his own as well. His clothes are a sweat-sponge. Yet he says not a word. Silence encloses him in its shield. The Sergeant eases back into his chair, and turns a little. The leather snaps as if he had been glued to it. Thomas answers for someone else in the room. A man with blood darker than the forest of his people. A Klallam elder he has sworn to his ancestors to honor with his name and his life.

"My father's a white sailor and my mother an American Indian, sir."

Irritated and reflecting disappointment, the Sergeant shouts.

"It's about time ya' answered me, boy. But how many goddamn times I got to tell you to speak loud and clear. I'm deaf, ya' got to holler it out."

"Yes, sir! My mother's Indian and my father white."

"I didn't hear a word you said. You must have a mouth full of shit."

"Can't you, Sir!"

"So, your father never swam the Rio Grande. Too fucking bad. He should'a. Down home where I come from we fry niggers like ya' in chicken fat and feed the remains to the hogs. Ya' know that?"

Thomas calls secretly to Cedar Crow; the chant his grandfather gave him as a child.

(When the world's too broken in spirit and has lost its heart, live in the cave inside your skull: follow hummingbird's flight through the yellow light to the center of our birth. Lie like an agate on the beach. Wait for wolf and eagle to lead you home.)

"No, sir."

Thomas steps with his grandfather down the path into the notice; his mind wears the shadows of this mountain clearing like a headband. Although fear and anger make a war inside his gut, he does not take his eyes from the wall.

"You can't tell me you were born in this country, boy. Americans know how to obey orders. After thumbing through your records, this leaves you out of the ball game. You've been a fuck-up left and right since boot camp from what I hear. All the time causing trouble, breaking every rule."

Thomas returns from the clearing; the sweat forms like oil beads and rolls down his forehead to his nose and lips. His eyes blink rapidly a few times, but never leave the wall. He sighs. He watches from behind the bear grass and giant ferns, the circle of dancers at Old Tillicum's last potlatch in 1891. Quickly, as if the sea had offered its cold but clear light, his mind takes the path back to it. On the coastal beach of his ancestors, he watches a family of Killer Whales surface and fall back into the water.

"Yes, sir, I mean, no sir."

Once more the seated man fondles his pencil, pushes back his chair, and looks away from Thomas. Faint clicks echo off the walls. He heaves himself from behind the desk and abruptly exits the room. He returns almost immediately, wiping cold water from his lips; he steps close to Thomas, smiles.

"You don't know what ya' mean, do you, boy? You're such a stupid retard, ya' probably couldn't find your way to the shitter, if your ass was chained to the stool. Shit, all ya' can say is yes sir and no, sir. Isn't that right, boy?"

"Yes, sir."

"What? Somebody cut out your tongue before I could? Those weren't words, punk."

"YES, SIR! YES, SIR!"

"All right, all right. Jesus Christ, give me a break. That's enough. So the cat ain't got your tongue. You're just an idiot in gorilla-wear."

"Yes, sir."

The Sergeant leans forward, digging for the way to look through Thomas.

"Now let me hear you say real loud, 'I'm the camp idiot, sir!'"

"You're . . . I mean, I'm the camp idiot, Sir!"

"Shit, I'm sick of looking at your ugly face, boy. I'm going to kick your ass into the deepest and rottenest hole we have here. You bore the piss out of me. From here on out, you're not Young Thomas anymore; you're Thirty. And if you don't want to end up at Sick Call, you fucking well better answer to Thirty. Turnkey! Turnkey! Get this piece of shit out of my sight before I puke!"

Yellow Eyes, a bald eagle, rises from the top of a red cedar, upward to the mountain peaks of Thomas's ancestors, returning to the Elwha River and its source. The steady keen of Eagle sweeps through Thomas. Thanking his guardian spirit, his grandfather, the people, and the dawn striking its story into the undulating coastal waters, he stands easily within the steel bars that surround the room. Yellow Eyes drifts over the room and glides downwind into the alpine clouds, and vanishes.

BORDERS (1993)

Thomas King

Thomas Hunt King was born in Roseville, California, in 1943. His father was Cherokee. King earned his Ph.D. in literature from the University of Utah and in 2012 retired from his job as a professor at Guelph University in Ontario. "Borders" appears in his collection, *One Good Story, That One*, which was a bestseller in Canada. Similarly to some of King's other stories, the plot focuses on the farcical nature of legal technicalities, narrated in this instance by a preadolescent boy: "It would have been easier if my mother had just said 'Canadian' and been done with it, but I could see she wasn't going to do that."

WHEN I WAS twelve, maybe thirteen, my mother announced that we were going to go to Salt Lake City to visit my sister who had left the reserve, moved across the state line, and found a job. Laetitia had not left home with my mother's blessing, but over time my mother had come to be proud of the fact that Laetitia had done all of this on her own.

"She did real good," my mother would say.

Then there were the fine points to Laetitia's going. She had not, as my mother liked to tell Mrs. Manyfingers, gone floating after some man like a balloon on a string. She hadn't snuck out of the house, either, and gone to Vancouver or Edmonton or Toronto to chase rainbows down alleys. And she hadn't been pregnant.

"She did real good."

I was seven or eight when Laetitia left home. She was seventeen. Our father was from Rocky Boy on the American side.

"Dad's American," Laetitia told my mother, "so I can go and come as I please."

"Send us a postcard."

Laetitia packed her things, and we headed for the border. Just outside of Milk River, Laetitia told us to watch for the water tower.

"Over the next rise. It's the first thing you see."

"We got a watch tower on the reserve," my mother said. "There's a big one in Lethbridge, too."

"You'll be able to see the tops of the flagpoles, too. That's where the border is."

When we got to Coutts, my mother stopped at the convenience store and bought her and Laetitia a cup of coffee. I got an Orange Crush.

"This is real lousy coffee."

"You're just angry because I want to see the world."

"It's the water. From here on down, they got lousy water."

"I can catch the bus from Sweetgrass. You don't have to lift a finger."

"You're going to have to buy your water in bottles if you want good coffee."

There was an old wooden building about a block away, with a tall sign in the yard that said "Museum." Most of the roof had been blown away. Mom told me to go and see when the place was open. There were boards over the windows and doors. You could tell that the place was closed, and I told Mom so, but she said to go and check anyway. Mom and Laetitia stayed by the car. Neither one of them moved. I sat down on the steps of the museum and watched them, and I don't know that they ever said anything to each other. Finally, Laetitia got her bag out of the trunk and gave Mom a hug.

I wandered back to the car. The wind had come up, and it blew Laetitia's hair across her face. Mom reached out and pulled the strands out of Laetitia's eyes, and Laetitia let her.

"You can see the mountain from here," my mother told Laetitia in Blackfoot.

"Lots of mountains in Salt Lake," Laetitia told her in English.

"The place is closed," I said. "Just like I told you."

Laetitia tucked her hair into her jacket and dragged her bag down the road to the brick building with the American flag flapping on a pole. When she got to where the guards were waiting, she turned, put the bag down, and waved to us. We waved back. Then my mother turned the car around, and we came home.

We got postcards from Laetitia regular, and, if she wasn't spreading jelly on the truth, she was happy. She found a good job and rented an apartment with a pool.

"And she can't even swim," my mother told Mrs. Manyfingers.

Most of the postcards said we should come down and see the city, but whenever I mentioned this, my mother would stiffen up.

So I was surprised when she bought two new tires for the car and put on her blue dress with the green and yellow flowers. I had to dress up, too, for my mother did not want us crossing the border looking like Americans. We made sandwiches and put them in a big box with pop and potato chips and some apples and bananas and a big jar of water.

"But we can stop at one of those restaurants, too, right?"

"We maybe should take some blankets in case you get sleepy."

"But we can stop at one of those restaurants, too, right?"

The border was actually two towns, though neither one was big enough to amount to anything. Coutts was on the Canadian side and consisted of the convenience store and gas station, the museum that was closed and boarded up, and a motel. Sweetgrass was on the American side, but all you could see was an overpass that arched across the highway and disappeared into the prairies. Just hearing the names of these towns, you would expect that Sweetgrass, which is a nice name and sounds like it is related to other places such as Medicine Hat and Moose Jaw and Kicking Horse Pass, would be on the Canadian side, and that Coutts, which sounds abrupt and rude, would be on the American side. But this was not the case.

Between the two borders was a duty-free shop where you could buy cigarettes and liquor and flags. Stuff like that.

We left the reserve in the morning and drove until we got to Coutts.

"Last time we stopped here," my mother said, "you had an Orange Crush. You remember that?"

"Sure," I said. "That was when Laetitia took off."

"You want another Orange Crush?"

"That means we're not going to stop at a restaurant, right?"

My mother got a coffee at the convenience store, and we stood around and watched the prairies move in the sunlight. Then we climbed back in the car. My mother straightened the dress across her thighs, leaned against the wheel, and drove all the way to the border in first gear, slowly, as if she were trying to see through a bad storm or riding high on black ice.

The border guard was an old guy. As he walked to the car, he swayed from side to side, his feet set wide apart, the holster on his hip pitching up and down. He leaned into the window, looked into the back seat, and looked at my mother and me.

"Morning, ma'am."

"Good morning."

"Where you heading?"

"Salt Lake City."

"Purpose of your visit?"

"Visit my daughter."

"Citizenship?"

"Blackfoot," my mother told him.

"Ma'am?"

"Blackfoot," my mother repeated.

"Canadian?"

"Blackfoot."

It would have been easier if my mother had just said "Canadian" and been done with it, but I could see she wasn't going to do that. The guard wasn't angry or anything. He smiled and looked towards the building. Then he turned back and nodded.

"Morning, ma'am."

"Good morning."

"Any firearms or tobacco?"

"No."

"Citizenship?"

"Blackfoot."

He told us to sit in the car and wait, and we did. In about five minutes, another guard came out with the first man. They were talking as they came, both men swaying back and forth like two cowboys headed for a bar or a gunfight.

"Morning, ma'am."

"Good morning."

"Cecil tells me you and the boy are Blackfoot."

"That's right."

"Now, I know that we got Blackfeet on the American side and the Canadians got Blackfeet on their side. Just so we can keep our records straight, what side do you come from?"

I knew exactly what my mother was going to say, and I could have told them if they had asked me.

"Canadian side or American side?" asked the guard.

"Blackfoot side," she said.

It didn't take them long to lose their sense of humor, I can tell you that. The one guard stopped smiling altogether and told us to park our car at the side of the building and come in.

We sat on a wood bench for about an hour before anyone came over to talk to us. This time it was a woman. She had a gun, too.

"Hi," she said. "I'm Inspector Pratt. I understand there is a little misunderstanding."

"I'm going to visit my daughter in Salt Lake City," my mother told her. "We don't have any guns or beer."

"It's a legal technicality, that's all."

"My daughter's Blackfoot, too."

The woman opened a briefcase and took out a couple of forms and began to write on one of them. "Everyone who crosses our border has to declare their citizenship. Even Americans. It helps us keep track of the visitors we get from the various countries."

She went on like that for maybe fifteen minutes, and a lot of the stuff she told us was interesting.

"I can understand how you feel about having to tell us your citizenship, and here's what I'll do. You tell me, and I won't put it down on the form. No one will know but you and me."

Her gun was silver. There were several chips in the wood handle and the name "Stella" was scratched into the metal butt.

We were in the border office for about four hours, and we talked to almost everyone there. One of the men bought me a Coke. My mother brought a couple of sandwiches in from the car. I offered part of mine to Stella, but she said she wasn't hungry.

I told Stella that we were Blackfeet and Canadian, but she said that that didn't count because I was a minor. In the end, she told us that if my mother didn't declare her citizenship, we would have to go back to where we came from. My mother stood up and thanked Stella for her time. Then we got back in the car and drove to the Canadian border, which was only about a hundred yards away.

I was disappointed. I hadn't seen Laetitia for a long time, and I had never been to Salt Lake City. When she was still at home, Laetitia would go on and on about Salt Lake City. She had never been there, but her boyfriend Lester Tallbull had spent a year in Salt Lake at a technical school.

"It's a great place," Lester would say. "Nothing but blondes in the whole state."

Whenever he said that, Laetitia would slug him on his shoulder hard enough to make him flinch. He had some brochures on Salt

Lake and some maps, and every so often the two of them would spread them out on the table.

"That's the temple. It's right downtown. You got to have a pass to get in."

"Charlotte says anyone can go in and look around."

"When was Charlotte in Salt Lake? Just when the hell was Charlotte in Salt Lake?"

"Last year."

"This is Liberty Park. It's got a zoo. There's good skiing in the mountains."

"Got all the skiing we can use," my mother would say. "People come from all over the world to ski at Banff. Cardston's got a temple, if you like those kinds of things."

"Oh, this one is real big," Lester would say. "They got armed guards and everything."

"Not what Charlotte says."

"What does she know?"

Lester and Laetitia broke up, but I guess the idea of Salt Lake stuck in her mind.

The Canadian border guard was a young woman, and she seemed happy to see us. "Hi," she said. "You folks sure have a great day for a trip. Where are you coming from?"

"Standoff."

"Is that in Montana?"

"No."

"Where are you going?"

"Standoff."

The woman's name was Carol and I don't guess she was any older than Laetitia. "Wow, you both Canadians?"

"Blackfoot."

"Really? I have a friend I went to school with who is Blackfoot. Do you know Mike Harley?"

"No."

"He went to school in Lethbridge, but he's really from Browning."

It was a nice conversation and there were no cars behind us, so there was no rush.

"You're not bringing any liquor back, are you?"

"No."

"Any cigarettes or plants or stuff like that?"

"No."

"Citizenship?"

"Blackfoot."

"I know," said the woman, "and I'd be proud of being Blackfoot if I were Blackfoot. But you have to be American or Canadian."

When Laetitia and Lester broke up, Lester took his brochures and maps with him, so Laetitia wrote to someone in Salt Lake City, and, about a month later, she got a big envelope of stuff. We sat at the table and opened up all the brochures, and Laetitia read each one aloud.

"Salt Lake City is the gateway to some of the world's most magnificent skiing.

"Salt Lake City is the home of one of the newest professional basketball franchises, the Utah Jazz.

"The Great Salt Lake is one of the natural wonders of the world."

It was kind of exciting seeing all those color brochures on the table and listening to Laetitia read all about how Salt Lake City was one of the best places in the entire world.

"That Salt Lake City place sounds too good to be true," my mother told her.

"It has everything."

"We got everything right here."

"It's boring here."

"People in Salt Lake City are probably sending away for brochures of Calgary and Lethbridge and Pincher Creek right now."

In the end, my mother would say that maybe Laetitia should go to Salt Lake City, and Laetitia would say that maybe she would.

We parked the car to the side of the building and Carol led us into a small room on the second floor. I found a comfortable spot on the couch and flipped through some back issues of *Saturday Night* and *Alberta Report*.

When I woke up, my mother was just coming out of another office. She didn't say a word to me. I followed her down the stairs and out to the car. I thought we were going home, but she turned the car around and drove back towards the American border, which made me think we were going to visit Laetitia in Salt Lake City after all. Instead she pulled into the parking lot of the duty-free store and stopped.

"We going to see Laetitia?"

"No."

"We going home?"

Pride is a good thing to have, you know. Laetitia had a lot of pride, and so did my mother. I figured that someday, I'd have it, too.

"So where are we going?"

Most of that day, we wandered around the duty-free store, which wasn't very large. The manager had a name tag with a tiny American flag on one side and a tiny Canadian flag on the other. His name was Mel. Towards evening, he began suggesting that we should be on our way. I told him we had nowhere to go, that neither the Americans nor the Canadians would let us in. He laughed at that and told us that we should buy something or leave.

The car was not very comfortable, but we did have all that food and it was April, so even if it did snow as it sometimes does on the prairies, we wouldn't freeze. The next morning my mother drove to the American border.

It was a different guard this time, but the questions were the same. We didn't spend as much time in the office as we had the day before. By noon, we were back at the Canadian border. By two we were back in the duty-free shop parking lot.

The second night in the car was not as much fun as the first, but my mother seemed in good spirits, and, all in all, it was as much an adventure as an inconvenience. There wasn't much food left and that was a problem, but we had lots of water as there was a faucet at the side of the duty-free shop.

One Sunday, Laetitia and I were watching television. Mom was over at Mrs. Manyfingers's. Right in the middle of the program, Laetitia turned off the set and said she was going to Salt Lake City, that life around here was too boring. I had wanted to see the rest of the program and really didn't care if Laetitia went to Salt Lake City or not. When Mom got home, I told her what Laetitia had said.

What surprised me was how angry Laetitia got when she found out that I had told Mom.

"You got a big mouth."

"That's what you said."

"What I said is none of your business."

"I didn't say anything."

"Well, I'm going for sure, now."

That weekend, Laetitia packed her bags, and we drove her to the border.

Mel turned out to be friendly. When he closed up for the night and found us still parked in the lot, he came over and asked us if our car was broken down or something. My mother thanked him for his concern and told him that we were fine, that things would get straightened out in the morning.

"You're kidding," said Mel. "You'd think they could handle the simple things."

"We got some apples and a banana," I said, "but we're all out of ham sandwiches."

"You know, you read about these things, but you just don't believe it. You just don't believe it."

"Hamburgers would be even better because they got more stuff for energy."

My mother slept in the back seat. I slept in the front because I was smaller and could lie under the steering wheel. Late that night, I heard my mother open the car door. I found her sitting on her blanket leaning against the bumper of the car.

"You see all those stars," she said. "When I was a little girl, my grandmother used to take me and my sisters out on the prairies and tell us stories about all the stars."

"Do you think Mel is going to bring us any hamburgers?"

"Every one of those stars has a story. You see that bunch of stars over there that look like a fish?"

"He didn't say no."

"Coyote went fishing, one day. That's how it all started." We sat out under the stars that night, and my mother told me all sorts of stories. She was serious about it, too. She'd tell them slow, repeating parts as she went, as if she expected me to remember each one.

Early the next morning, the television vans began to arrive, and guys in suits and women in dresses came trotting over to us, dragging microphones and cameras and lights behind them. One of the vans had a table set up with orange juice and sandwiches and fruit. It was for the crew, but when I told them we hadn't eaten for a while, a really skinny blonde woman told us we could eat as much as we wanted.

They mostly talked to my mother. Every so often one of the reporters would come over and ask me questions about how it felt to be an Indian without a country. I told them we had a nice house on the reserve and that my cousins had a couple of horses we rode when we went fishing. Some of the television people went over to the American border, and then they went to the Canadian border.

Around noon, a good-looking guy in a dark blue suit and an orange tie with little ducks on it drove up in a fancy car. He talked to my mother for a while, and, after they were done talking, my mother called me over, and we got into our car. Just as my mother started the engine, Mel came over and gave us a bag of peanut brittle and told us that justice was a damn hard thing to get, but that we shouldn't give up.

I would have preferred lemon drops, but it was nice of Mel anyway.

"Where are we going now?"

"Going to visit Laetitia."

The guard who came out to our car was all smiles. The television lights were so bright they hurt my eyes, and, if you tried to look through the windshield in certain directions, you couldn't see a thing.

"Morning, ma'am."

"Good morning."

"Where you heading?"

"Salt Lake City."

"Purpose of your visit?"

"Visit my daughter."

"Any tobacco, liquor, or firearms?"

"Don't smoke."

"Any plants or fruit?"

"Not any more."

"Citizenship?"

"Blackfoot."

The guard rocked back on his heels and jammed his thumbs into his gun belt. "Thank you," he said, his fingers patting the butt of the revolver. "Have a pleasant trip."

My mother rolled the car forward, and the television people had to scramble out of the way. They ran alongside the car as we pulled away from the border, and, when they couldn't run any farther, they stood in the middle of the highway and waved and waved and waved.

We got to Salt Lake City the next day. Laetitia was happy to see us, and, that first night, she took us out to a restaurant that made really good soups. The list of pies took up a whole page. I had cherry. Mom had chocolate. Laetitia said that she saw us on television the night before and, during the meal, she had us tell her the story over and over again.

Laetitia took us everywhere. We went to a fancy ski resort. We went to the temple. We got to go shopping in a couple of large malls, but they weren't as large as the one in Edmonton, and Mom said so.

After a week or so, I got bored and wasn't at all sad when my mother said we should be heading back home. Laetitia wanted us to stay longer, but Mom said no, that she had things to do back home and that, next time, Laetitia should come up and visit. Laetitia said she was thinking about moving back, and Mom told her to do as she pleased, and Laetitia said that she would.

On the way home, we stopped at the duty-free shop, and my mother gave Mel a green hat that said "Salt Lake" across the front. Mel was a funny guy. He took the hat and blew his nose and told my mother that she was an inspiration to us all. He gave us some more peanut brittle and came out into the parking lot and waved at us all the way to the Canadian border.

It was almost evening when we left Coutts. I watched the border through the rear window until all you could see were the tops of the flagpoles and the blue water tower, and then they rolled over a hill and disappeared.

THE DOG PIT (1994)

Eli Funaro

Funaro seems to hail from Minnesota, where he is a video director. This plain-spoken and shocking story was written for a program at the Institute of American Indian Arts in Santa Fe.

IT WAS A sunny Saturday, the day that dog died. My pop snapped me outta unconsciousness with a reminder of Garbage Day.

"Get your butt up," he said. "I wanna get to the dump before noon."

"Aw jeez," I mumbled, wiping the cheese out of my eyes. "Why we going so early?"

"Cuz I gotta work at three," he said. "And I wanted to go to Bonimart."

Quickly I got up and ate my Fruit Loops. The thought of going to Bonimart brought high hopes of getting a new toy, and Zartan was well on my mind. I got dressed with enthusiasm and eagerly fetched the plastic Rubbermaid trash cans.

On the rez, there were no garbage trucks that came to pick up your trash. We had to haul our own to the dump. So like all the previous Saturdays, I loaded up the van with our garbage bins.

I found enough strength in my eight-year-old body to lift the barrels into the back of the van, even though they were about the same size as I was. And before I left, I filled my dog's dish with water and Kibbles 'n Bits.

"Here you go, Corky," I said as my black Labrador came to his bowl. I began to pet his neck. "Chow down."

"Hurry up, will ya?" my pop called from the van. "You fed that mutt yesterday."

"He's hungry," I said.

"He's always hungry," he replied. "Let's go, huh?"

I got into the van and my pop drove us off to the dump.

As we drove along the untitled roads I sat in the passenger seat fiddling through the glove compartment. There was a pink rubber sponge ball inside. I picked it up and bounced it around in my hands.

"You can have that," my pop said.

"Where'd you get it?" I asked.

"At work," he answered, and I wondered. My pop was a janitor at the hospital, so why would he get a ball from there?

"At work?" I said. "What are a bunch of balls doing at work?"

"Well," my pop explained, "I was in some room sweeping and there was an old man laying on the bed. He was just laying there and he was holding that ball."

"He gave it to you?" I asked.

"Sort of," he said. "The doctors sometimes have sick people squeeze them balls to see how strong they are, or to see if they're still alive." My pop laughed a little bit. "And that old man wasn't squeezing nothing."

"You mean he was dead?" I asked, twitching my nose.

He looked at me with an evil grin. "Yup."

"Yeeks!" I squealed, dropping the ball. He tried to give me a dead guy's ball. And I didn't want the guy's ghost coming after me. I just let it go.

"So I just grabbed it," my pop said. "Besides, what's a dead man gonna do with a ball?"

I didn't say anything. I just sat there staring at the ball, imagining what it was like to die holding it. I wondered how many balls the doctors gave to dead people and wondered if they got buried with them. I wondered if that old man would be mad at us for taking his ball. But my pop just sat there smiling as he drove.

The dump was in view and as we approached, the oddly familiar scent of burning trash embedded itself in our noses. Thick, black smoke crawled into the sky like oozing charcoal toothpaste. Seagulls flocked overhead, making their high-pitched yells. A breeze blew various debris about the waste.

The site was full of garbage mountains with dirt roads winding around the huge mounds. The flames of burning trash danced around the site. We found a space away from the other cars that parked throughout the dump throwing out their own waste. The rancid smell of decomposing garbage was everywhere.

I got out and opened the back door of the van. Arching backwards, I heaved the huge plastic barrel out of the van and dragged it to the edge of the mound. My pop grabbed the last two trash bins.

After they were empty we filled the bottom of each barrel with bleach. That would kill the rotten stench of a week-old garbage bag as well as kill the maggots that adopted the barrel as a nest.

The seagulls still flew around squeaking their voices above. We waited a few minutes for the Clorox to kick in. I gazed around the mountains of trash and noticed the other people who unloaded their garbage. I watched the flames of burning piles while pieces of junk blew around. I looked at the opened side door of the van and saw the pink ball sitting on the floor. I went to go and pick it up. While I sat on the bumper looking at the ball my pop came up to me.

"You know those are real good for playing baseball with," he said. "You could hit them real far."

I looked at him.

"Do you think that old man will be mad for taking his ball?"

"No," he laughed. "I don't think he was thinking too much about that ball when he keeled over. He couldn't even hold it. Why would he want to keep it?"

"Yeah, but what about all the other balls?" I asked. "Did the other dead people get to keep them?"

"No," he said. "I bet about twenty different people died holding that same ball."

I looked at the ball. Now it wouldn't only be one old man being mad, it was a whole cemetery. I put the ball down again.

A thunderclap exploded suddenly. It echoed throughout the sky, making the seagulls rave in a commotion. But under their high-pitched yells was a faint squeal. It came not from the sky but from the other side of the dump. My attention was drawn to an old white pick-up. An old man stood outside. He held a shotgun and pumped another round into the chamber. I stared curiously at what he was gonna shoot. It was a yellow pillow sack on the ground. The faint screams wallowed inside the bag.

I watched in amazement as the old man pointed the barrel at the wiggling sack. Another explosion echoed as the pillow case burst with red haze and pieces of cloth blew away. The seagulls spoke anxiously overhead.

I stared as the old man picked up the bloodstained pillow sack. He walked onto the lawn of garbage and tossed the bloody sack away. I looked at my pop.

"Did you see what that guy just did? He just shot something in that bag."

My pop looked back at me.

"He took his dog to the Pit."

"The Pit?" I asked. "What's that?"

"When your dog dies," he explained, "you throw it in the Pit. It's like a cemetery for pets."

"Yeah, but he shot it," I replied.

"If it's too old or dies," he said. "Whichever comes first. When my dog got too old, my dad shot him too. And he's in that Pit right now."

I looked back at the old man, who climbed in his beat-up pick-up and drove away. I walked across the dump, stumbling over junk and debris strewn all over the ground. The seagulls settled down somewhat and my pop began to load the trash cans back into the van.

As I walked toward the Pit, I saw a hole in the ground. There was a faint whimper coming from below. The hole was deep, about four feet in diameter. It was an old well.

I stood at the edge of the Pit and stared down. About thirty feet deep there was a pile. It wasn't garbage but the remains of dead pets. Bodies of half-rancid dogs. Bones and fur covered with maggots. Skulls decaying with rotten hides. And on top of the pile was the bloody pillow case that still wiggled slowly. Faint low whimpers came from below the rotting mound, surrounded by the cryptic brick walls of the well, all dusty and covered with cobwebs.

I was shocked and impressed by the sight below me. The pillow case vibrated with lagging reflex as the whining died. The movements slowed to a halt. The pillow case was still and never moved again.

"Hey, let's go!"

I turned around and saw the van on the side of the dirt road. My pop was waiting inside. I ran to the truck and we took off.

"So what do you think of the Dog Pit?" my pop asked.

"When Corky dies," I wondered, "is he going down there too?"

"Well," he said, "if you want, we could bury him in the backyard, but Corky ain't gonna die for a long time, so quit worrying."

I saw the pink rubber ball and picked it up again. I wondered what it would be like to be down there. Rotting with all the rest of them bones. Bugs and worms crawling all over. Covered by a bunch of dead bodies.

As we drove down the road, I took a glance into the rearview mirror. The flames of the garbage fires still crept into the sky and the scent still lingered in the air. I looked back at the pink rubber ball, squeezing it around my palm. I wish I'd never seen the Pit.

Still we drove away and we later went to Bonimart. My pop bought me Zartan along with Stormshadow, which kept me busy for hours creating my own stories of death. And the events of the day were soon forgotten with short memory.

BEADING LESSON (2002)

Beth H. Piatote

Piatote is Nez Perce and a professor of Native American Studies at the University of California, Berkeley. She is the author of *Domestic Subjects: Gender, Citizenship, and Law in Native American Literature* (Yale).

THE FIRST THING you do is, lay down all your hanks, like this, so the colors go from light to dark, like a rainbow. I'll start you out with something real easy, like I do with those kids over at the school, over at Cay-Uma-Wa.

How about—you want to make some earrings for your mama? Yeah, I think she would like that.

Hey niece, you remind me of those kids. That's good! That's good to be thinking of your mama.

You go ahead and pick some colors you think she would like. Maybe three or four is all, and you need to pick some of these bugle beads.

Yeah, that's good, except you got too many dark colors.

You like dark colors. Every time I see you you're wearin' something dark. Not me. I like to wear red and yellow, so people know I'm around and don't try talkin' about me behind my back, aay?

The thing is, you got to use some light colors, because you're makin' these for your mama, right, and she has dark hair, and you want 'em to stand out, and if they're all dark colors you can't see the pattern.

I got some thread for you, and this beeswax. You cut the thread about this long, a little longer than your arm, but you don't want it too long or it will tangle up or get real weak. You run it through

100

the beeswax, like this, until it's just about straight. It makes it strong and that way it don't tangle so much.

You keep all this in your box now. I got this for you to take home with you, back to college, so you can keep doin' your beadwork.

How do you like it over there at the university? You know your cousin Rae is just about gettin' her degree. She just has her practicum, then she'll be done. I think her boyfriend don't like her being in school though, and that's slowing her down. It's probably a good thing you don't have a boyfriend right now. They can really make a lot of trouble for you, and slow you down on things you got to do.

Now you gotta watch this part. This is how you make the knot. You make a circle like this, then you wrap the thread around the needle three times, see? You see how my hands are? If you forget later you just remember how my hands are, just like this, and remember you have to make a circle, OK? Then you pull the needle through all the way to the end—good—and clip off the little tail.

I'll show you these real easy earrings, the same thing I always start those men at the jail with. You know I go over there and give them beading lessons. You should see how artistic some of them are. They work real hard, and some of them are good at beadwork.

I guess they got a lot of time to do it, but it's hard, it's hard to do real good beadwork.

You got to go slow and pay attention.

I know this one man, William, he would be an artist if he wasn't in jail. I'll show you, he gave me a drawing he did of an eagle. It could be a photograph, except you can tell it's just pencil. But it's good, you would like it. There's a couple of other Indian prisoners—I guess we're supposed to call them inmates, but I always call them prisoners—and sometimes I make designs for them for their beadwork from what they draw. The thing is, they don't get many colors to work with.

They like the beadwork, though. They always got something to give their girlfriends when they come visit, or their mothers and aunties.

You have to hide the knot in the bead, see, like this, and that's why you got to be careful not to make the knot too big.

Maybe next time you come they will be having a powwow at the prison and you can meet my students over there and they can show you their beadwork. I think they always have a powwow around November, around Veterans Day. Your cousin Carlisle and his family come over from Montana last time, and the only thing is, you got to go real early because it takes a long time to get all your things through security. They have to check all your regalia and last time they almost wouldn't let Carlisle take his staff in because they said it was too dangerous or something.

What's that? Oh, that's all right. Just make it the same way on the other one and everyone will think you did it that way on purpose.

Your mama is really going to like those earrings. I think sometimes she wishes she learnt to bead, but she didn't want to when she was little. She was the youngest, so I think she was a little spoiled but don't tell her I said that. She didn't have to do things she didn't want to, she didn't even have to go to boarding school. I think she would have liked it. It wasn't bad for me at that school. Those nuns were good to me; they doted on me. I was their pet. I think your mama missed out on something, not going to St. Andrew's, because that's when you get real close with other Indians.

I like that blue. I think I'm goin' to make you a wing dress that color.

I think you'll look good when you're ready to dance. Once you get going on your beadwork I'll get you started on your moccasins, and you know your cousin Woody is making you a belt and I know this lady who can make you a cornhusk bag. You're goin' to look just like your mama did when she was young, except I think she was younger than you the last time she put on beadwork.

I used to wonder if you would look like your dad, but now that you're grown you sure took after her. I look at you and I think my sister, she must have some strong blood.

Hey, you're doin' real good there, niece. I think you got "the gift"—good eyesight! You know, you always got to be workin' on something, because people are always needing things for weddin's and memorials and going out the first time, got to get their outfits together. Most everything I make I give away, but people pay me to make special things. And they are always askin' for my work at the gift shop. My beadwork has got me through some hard times, some years of livin' skinny.

You got to watch out for some people, though. Most people aren't like this; most people are real big-hearted. But some people, when they buy your beadwork, they think it should last forever. Somebody's car breaks down, he knows he got to take it to the shop, pay someone to get it goin' again. But not with beadwork— not with something an Indian made. No, they bring it back ten years later and they want you to fix it for free! They think because an Indian makes it, it's got to last forever. Just think if the Indians did that with all the things the government made for us. Hey, you got to fix it for free!

You done with that already? Let me show you how you finish. You pull the thread through this line, see, then clip it, then the bead covers it up. That's nice.

That's good. I'm proud of you, niece.

I think your mama is really goin' to like these earrings, and maybe she'll come and ask you to teach her how you do it. You think she'll ever want to learn beadwork? Maybe she'll come and ask me, aay?

What do you think of that? You think your mama would ever want to learn something from her big sister? I got a lot of students. There's a lady who just called me the other day, she works at the health clinic, and she's older than you and she wants to learn how. I said sure I'll teach her. I teach anyone who wants to learn. I just keep thinkin' if I stay around long enough, everyone's goin' to come back and ask me, even your mama.

WAR DANCES (2009)

Sherman Alexie

Born in 1966, of Coeur d'Alene and Spokane heritage, Alexie has been publishing poems and fiction since 1993. He is the most colloquial of writers in this anthology, writing with a confessional voice that is often humorous. His books have won many awards; he adapted his early stories for the movie *Smoke Signals* (1998). The strange, great, and discursive "War Dances" is the title story of one of his recent collections of short fiction.

1. My Kafka Baggage

A few years ago, after I returned from a trip to Los Angeles, I unpacked my bag and found a dead cockroach, shrouded by a dirty sock, in a bottom corner. "Shit," I thought. "We're being invaded." And so I threw the unpacked clothes, books, shoes, and toiletries back into the suitcase, carried it out onto the driveway, and dumped the contents onto the pavement, ready to stomp on any other cockroach stowaways. But there was only the one cockroach, stiff and dead. As he lay on the pavement, I leaned closer to him. His legs were curled under his body. His head was tilted at a sad angle. Sad? Yes, sad. For who is lonelier than the cockroach without his tribe? I laughed at myself. I was feeling empathy for a dead cockroach. I wondered about its story. How had it got into my bag? And where? At the hotel in Los Angeles? In an airport baggage system? It didn't originate in our house. We've kept those tiny bastards away from our place for fifteen years. So what had happened to this little vermin? Did he smell something delicious in my bag—my musky deodorant or some crumb of chocolate Power Bar—and climb inside, only to be crushed by the shifts of fate and garment bags? As he died did he feel fear? Isolation? Existential dread?

2. Symptoms

Last summer, in reaction to various allergies I was suffering from, defensive mucus flooded my inner right ear and confused, frightened, untied, and unmoored me. Simply stated, I could not fucking hear a thing from that side, so I had to turn my head to understand what my two sons, ages eight and ten, were saying.

"We're hungry," they said. "We keep telling you."

They wanted to be fed. And I had not heard them.

"Mom would have fed us by now," they said.

Their mother had left for Italy with her mother two days ago. My sons and I were going to enjoy a boys' week, filled with unwashed socks, REI rock wall climbing, and ridiculous heaps of pasta.

"What are you going to cook?" my sons asked. "Why haven't you cooked yet?"

I'd been lying on the couch reading a book while they played and I had not realized that I'd gone partially deaf. So I, for just a moment, could only weakly blame the silence—no, the contradictory roar that only I could hear.

Then I recalled the man who went to the emergency room because he'd woken having lost most, if not all, of his hearing. The doctor peered into one ear, saw an obstruction, reached in with small tweezers, and pulled out a cockroach, then reached into the other ear, and extracted a much larger cockroach. Did you know that ear wax is a delicacy for roaches?

I cooked dinner for my sons—overfed them out of guilt—and cleaned the hell out of our home. Then I walked into the bathroom and stood close to my mirror. I turned my head and body at weird angles, and tried to see deeply into my congested ear. I sang hymns and prayed that I'd see a small angel trapped in the canal. I would free the poor thing, and she'd unfurl and pat dry her tiny wings, then fly to my lips and give me a sweet kiss for sheltering her metamorphosis.

3. The Symptoms Worsen

When I woke at three a.m., completely unable to hear out of my clogged right ear and positive that a damn swarm of locusts was wedged inside, I left a message for my doctor, and told him that I would be sitting outside his office when he reported to work.

This would be the first time I had been inside a health-care facility since my father's last surgery.

4. Blankets

After the surgeon cut off my father's right foot—no, half of my father's right foot—and three toes from the left, I sat with him in the recovery room. It was more like a recovery hallway. There was no privacy, not even a thin curtain. I guessed it made it easier for the nurses to monitor the postsurgical patients, but still, my father was exposed—his decades of poor health and worse decisions were illuminated—on white sheets in a white hallway under white lights.

"Are you okay?" I asked. It was a stupid question. Who could be okay after such a thing? Yesterday, my father had *walked* into the hospital. Okay, he'd shuffled while balanced on two canes, but that was still called walking. A few hours ago, my father still had both of his feet. Yes, his feet and toes had been black with rot and disease but they'd still been, technically speaking, feet and toes. And, most important, those feet and toes had belonged to my father. But now they were gone, sliced off. Where were they? What did they do with the right foot and the toes from the left foot? Did they throw them in the incinerator? Were their ashes floating over the city?

"Doctor, I'm cold," my father said.

"Dad, it's me," I said.

"I know who are you. You're my son." But considering the blankness in my father's eyes, I assumed he was just guessing at my identity.

"Dad, you're in the hospital. You just had surgery."

"I know where I am. I'm cold."

"Do you want another blanket?" Another stupid question. Of course, he wanted another blanket. He probably wanted me to build a fucking campfire or drag in one of those giant propane heaters that NFL football teams used on the sidelines.

I walked down the hallway—the recovery hallway—to the nurses' station. There were three women nurses, two white and one black. Being Native American-Spokane and Coeur d'Alene Indian, I hoped my darker pigment would give me an edge with the black nurse, so I addressed her directly.

"My father is cold," I said. "Can I get another blanket?"

The black nurse glanced up from her paperwork and regarded me. Her expression was neither compassionate nor callous.

"How can I help you, sir?" she asked.

"I'd like another blanket for my father. He's cold."

"I'll be with you in a moment, sir."

She looked back down at her paperwork. She made a few notes. Not knowing what else to do, I stood there and waited.

"Sir," the black nurse said. "I'll be with you in a moment."

She was irritated. I understood. After all, how many thousands of times had she been asked for an extra blanket? She was a nurse, an educated woman, not a damn housekeeper. And it was never really about an extra blanket, was it? No, when people asked for an extra blanket, they were asking for a time machine. And, yes, she knew she was a health care provider, and she knew she was supposed to be compassionate, but my father, an alcoholic, diabetic Indian with terminally damaged kidneys, had just endured an incredibly expensive surgery for what? So he could ride his motorized wheelchair to the bar and win bets by showing off his disfigured foot? I know she didn't want to be cruel, but she believed there was a point when doctors should stop rescuing people from their own self-destructive impulses. And I couldn't disagree with her but I could ask for the most basic of comforts, couldn't I?

"My father," I said. "An extra blanket, please."

"Fine," she said, then stood and walked back to a linen closet, grabbed a white blanket, and handed it to me. "If you need anything else—"

I didn't wait around for the end of her sentence. With the blanket in hand, I walked back to my father. It was a thin blanket, laundered and sterilized a hundred times. In fact, it was too thin. It wasn't really a blanket. It was more like a large beach towel. Hell, it wasn't even good enough for that. It was more like the world's largest coffee filter. Jesus, had health care finally come to this? Everybody was uninsured and unblanketed.

"Dad, I'm back."

He looked so small and pale lying in that hospital bed. How had that change happened? For the first sixty-seven years of his life, my father had been a large and dark man. And now, he was just another pale and sick drone in a hallway of pale and sick drones. A hive, I thought, this place looks like a beehive with colony collapse disorder.

"Dad, it's me."

"I'm cold."

"I have a blanket."

As I draped it over my father and tucked it around his body, I felt the first sting of grief. I'd read the hospital literature about this moment. There would come a time when roles would reverse and the adult child would become the caretaker of the ill parent. The circle of life. Such poetic bullshit.

"I can't get warm," my father said. "I'm freezing."

"I brought you a blanket, Dad, I put it on you."

"Get me another one. Please. I'm so cold. I need another blanket."

I knew that ten more of these cheap blankets wouldn't be enough. My father needed a real blanket, a good blanket.

I walked out of the recovery hallway and made my way through various doorways and other hallways, peering into the rooms, looking at the patients and their families, looking for a particular kind of patient and family.

I walked through the ER, cancer, heart and vascular, neuroscience, orthopedic, women's health, pediatrics, and surgical services. Nobody stopped me. My expression and posture was that of a man with a sick father and so I belonged.

And then I saw him, another Native man, leaning against a wall near the gift shop. Well, maybe he was Asian; lots of those in Seattle. He was a small man, pale brown, with muscular arms and a soft belly. Maybe he was Mexican, which is really a kind of Indian, too, but not the kind that I needed. It was hard to tell sometimes what people were. Even brown people guessed at the identity of other brown people.

"Hey," I said.

"Hey," the other man said.

"You Indian?" I asked.

"Yeah."

"What tribe?"

"Lummi."

"I'm Spokane."

"My first wife was Spokane. I hated her."

"My first wife was Lummi. She hated me."

We laughed at the new jokes that instantly sounded old.

"Why are you in here?" I asked.

"My sister is having a baby," he said. "But don't worry, it's not mine."

"Ayyyyyy," I said—another Indian idiom—and laughed.

"I don't even want to be here," the other Indian said. "But my dad started, like, this new Indian tradition. He says it's a thousand years old. But that's bullshit. He just made it up to impress himself. And the whole family just goes along, even when we know it's bullshit. He's in the delivery room waving eagle feathers around. Jesus."

"What's the tradition?"

"Oh, he does a naming ceremony right in the hospital. Like, it's supposed to protect the baby from all the technology and shit. Like hospitals are the big problem. You know how many babies died before we had good hospitals?"

"I don't know."

"Most of them. Well, shit, a lot of them, at least."

This guy was talking out of his ass. I liked him immediately.

"I mean," the guy said. "You should see my dad right now. He's pretending to go into this, like, fucking trance and is dancing around my sister's bed, and he says he's trying to, you know, see into her womb, to see who the baby is, to see its true nature, so he can give it a name—a protective name—before it's born."

The guy laughed and threw his head back and banged it on the wall.

"I mean, come on, I'm a loser," he said and rubbed his sore skull. "My whole family is filled with losers."

The Indian world is filled with charlatans, men and women who pretended—hell, who might have come to believe—that they were holy. Last year, I had gone to a lecture at the University of Washington. An elderly Indian woman, a Sioux writer and scholar and charlatan, had come to orate on Indian sovereignty and literature. She kept arguing for some kind of separate indigenous literary identity, which was ironic considering that she was speaking English to a room full of white professors. But I wasn't angry with the woman, or even bored.

No, I felt sorry for her. I realized that she was dying of nostalgia. She had taken nostalgia as her false idol—her thin blanket—and it was murdering her.

"Nostalgia," I said to the other Indian man in the hospital.

"What?"

"Your dad, he sounds like he's got a bad case of nostalgia."

"Yeah, I hear you catch that from fucking old high school girl-friends," the man said. "What the hell you doing here anyway?"

"My dad just got his feet cut off," I said.

"Diabetes?"

"And vodka."

"Vodka straight up or with a nostalgia chaser?"

"Both."

"Natural causes for an Indian."

"Yep."

There wasn't much to say after that.

"Well I better get back," the man said. "Otherwise, my dad might wave an eagle feather and change my name."

"Hey, wait," I said.

"Yeah?"

"Can I ask you a favor?"

"What?"

"My dad, he's in the recovery room," I said. "Well it's more like a hallway, and he's freezing, and they've only got these shitty little blankets, and I came looking for Indians in the hospital because I figured—well, I guessed if I found any Indians, they might have some good blankets."

"So you want to borrow a blanket from us?" the man asked.

"Yeah."

"Because you thought some Indian would just have some extra blankets lying around?"

"Yeah."

"That's fucking ridiculous."

"I know."

"And it's racist."

"I know."

"You're stereotyping your own damn people."

"I know."

"But damn if we don't have a room full of Pendleton blankets. New ones. Jesus, you'd think my sister was having, like, a dozen babies."

Five minutes later, carrying a Pendleton Star Blanket, the Indian man walked out of his sister's hospital room, accompanied by his father, who wore Levi's, a black T-shirt, and eagle feathers in his gray braids.

"We want to give your father this blanket," the old man said. "It was meant for my grandson, but I think it will be good for your father, too."

"Thank you."

"Let me bless it. I will sing a healing song for the blanket. And for your father."

I flinched. This guy wanted to sing a song? That was dangerous. This song could take two minutes or two hours. It was impossible to know. Hell, considering how desperate this old man was to be seen as holy, he might sing for a week. I couldn't let this guy begin his song without issuing a caveat.

"My dad," I said, "I really need to get back to him. He's really sick."

"Don't worry," the old man said and winked. "I'll sing one of my short ones."

Jesus, who'd ever heard of a self-aware fundamentalist? The son, perhaps not the unbeliever he'd pretended to be, sang backup as his father launched into his radio-friendly honor song, just three-and-a-half minutes, like the length of any Top 40 rock song of the last fifty years. But here's the funny thing: the old man couldn't sing very well. If you were going to have the balls to sing healing songs in hospital hallways, then you should logically have a great voice, right? But, no, this guy couldn't keep the tune. And his voice cracked and wavered. Does a holy song lose its power if its singer is untalented?

"That is your father's song," the old man said when he was finished. "I give it to him. I will never sing it again. It belongs to your father now."

Behind his back, the old man's son rolled his eyes and walked back into his sister's room.

"Okay, thank you," I said.

I felt like an ass, accepting the blanket and the old man's good wishes, but silently mocking them at the same time. But maybe the old man did have some power, some real medicine, because he peeked into my brain.

"It doesn't matter if you believe in the healing song," the old man said. "It only matters that the blanket heard."

"Where have you been?" my father asked when I returned.

"I'm cold."

"I know, I know," I said. "I found you a blanket. A good one. It will keep you warm."

I draped the Star Blanket over my father. He pulled the thick wool up to his chin. And then he began to sing. It was a healing song, not the same song that I had just heard, but a healing song nonetheless. My father could sing beautifully. I wondered if it was proper for a man to sing a healing song for himself. I wondered if my father needed help with the song. I hadn't sung for many years, not like that, but I joined him. I knew this song would not bring back my father's feet. This song would not repair my father's bladder, kidneys, lungs, and heart. This song would not prevent my father from drinking a bottle of vodka as soon as he could sit up in bed. This song would not defeat death. No, I thought, this song is temporary, but right now, temporary is good enough. And it was a good song. Our voices filled the recovery hallway. The sick and healthy stopped to listen. The nurses, even the remote black one, unconsciously took a few steps toward us. The black nurse sighed and smiled. I smiled back. I knew what she was thinking. Sometimes, even after all of these years, she could still be surprised by her work. She still marveled at the infinite and ridiculous faith of other people.

5. Doctor's Office

I took my kids with me to my doctor, a handsome man—a reservist—who'd served in both Iraq wars. I told him I could not hear. He said his nurse would likely have to clear wax and fluid, but when he scoped inside, he discovered nothing.

"Nope, it's all dry in there," he said.

He led my sons and me to the audiologist in the other half of the building. I was scared, but I wanted my children to remain calm, so I tried to stay measured. More than anything, I wanted my wife to materialize.

During the hearing test, I heard only 30 percent of the clicks, bells, and words—I apparently had nerve and bone conductive deafness. My inner ear thumped and thumped.

How many cockroaches were in my head?

My doctor said, "We need an MRI of your ear and brain, and maybe we'll find out what's going on."

Maybe? That word terrified me.

What the fuck was wrong with my fucking head? Had my hydrocephalus come back for blood? Had my levees burst?

Was I going to flood?

6. Hydrocephalus

Merriam-Webster's dictionary defines hydrocephalus as "an abnormal increase in the amount of cerebrospinal fluid within the cranial cavity that is accompanied by expansion of the cerebral ventricles, enlargement of the skull and especially the forehead, and atrophy of the brain." I define hydrocephalus as "the obese, imperialistic water demon that nearly killed me when I was six months old."

In order to save my life, and stop the water demon, I had brain surgery in 1967 when I was six months old. I was supposed to die. Obviously, I didn't. I was supposed to be severely mentally disabled. I have only minor to moderate brain damage. I was supposed to have epileptic seizures. Those I did have, until I was seven years old. I was on phenobarbital, a major league antiseizure medication, for six years.

Some of the side effects of phenobarbital—all of which I suffered to some degree or another as a child—include sleepwalking, agitation, confusion, depression, nightmares, hallucinations, insomnia, apnea, vomiting, constipation, dermatitis, fever, liver and bladder dysfunction, and psychiatric disturbance.

How do you like them cockroaches?

And now, as an adult, thirty-three years removed from phenobarbital, I still suffer—to one degree or another—from sleepwalking, agitation, confusion, depression, nightmares, hallucinations, insomnia, bladder dysfunction, apnea, and dermatitis.

Is there such a disease as post-phenobarbital traumatic stress syndrome?

Most hydrocephalics are shunted. A shunt is essentially brain plumbing that drains away excess cerebrospinal fluid. Those shunts often fuck up and stop working. I know hydrocephalics who've had a hundred or more shunt revisions and repairs. That's over a hundred brain surgeries. There are ten fingers on any surgeon's hand. There are two or three surgeons working on any particular brain. That means certain hydrocephalics have had their brains fondled by three thousand fingers.

I'm lucky. I was only temporarily shunted. And I hadn't suffered any hydrocephalic symptoms since I was seven years old.

And then, in July 2008, at the age of forty-one, I went deaf in my right ear.

7. Conversation

Sitting in my car in the hospital parking garage, I called my brother-in-law, who was babysitting my sons.

"Hey, it's me. I just got done with the MRI on my head."

My brother-in-law said something unintelligible. I realized I was holding my cell to my bad ear. And switched it to the good ear.

"The MRI dude didn't look happy," I said.

"That's not good," my brother-in-law said.

"No, it's not. But he's just a tech guy, right? He's not an expert on brains or anything. He's just the photographer, really. And he doesn't know anything about ears or deafness or anything, I don't think. Ah, hell, I don't know what he knows. I just didn't like the look on his face when I was done."

"Maybe he just didn't like you."

"Well, I got worried when I told him I had hydrocephalus when I was a baby and he didn't seem to know what that was."

"Nobody knows what that is."

"That's the truth. Have you fed the boys dinner?"

"Yeah, but I was scrounging. There's not much here."

"I better go shopping."

"Are you sure? I can do it if you need me to. I can shop the shit out of Trader Joe's."

"No, it'll be good for me. I feel good. I fell asleep during the MRI. And I kept twitching. So we had to do it twice. Otherwise, I would've been done earlier."

"That's okay; I'm okay; the boys are okay."

"You know, before you go in that MRI tube, they ask you what kind of music you want to listen to—jazz, classical, rock or country—and I remembered how my dad spent a lot of time in MRI tubes near the end of his life. So I was wondering what kind of music he always chose. I mean, he couldn't hear shit anyway by that time, but he still must have chosen something. And I wanted to choose the same thing he chose. So I picked country."

"Was it good country?"

"It was fucking Shania Twain and Faith Hill shit. I was hoping for George Jones or Loretta Lynn, or even some George Strait. Hell, I would've cried if they'd played Charley Pride or Freddy Fender."

"You wanted to hear the alcoholic Indian father jukebox."

"Hey, that's my line. You can't quote me to me."

"Why not? You're always quoting you to you."

"Kiss my ass. So, hey, I'm okay, I think. And I'm going to the store. But I think I already said that. Anyway, I'll see you in a bit. You want anything?"

"Ah, man, I love Trader Joe's. But you know what's bad about them? You fall in love with something they have—they stock it for a year—and then it just disappears. They had those wontons I loved and now they don't. I was willing to shop for you and the boys, but I don't want anything for me. I'm on a one-man hunger strike against them."

8. World Phone Conversation, 3 a.m.

After I got home with yogurt and turkey dogs and Cinnamon Toast Crunch and my brother-in-law had left, I watched George Romero's *Diary of the Dead*, and laughed at myself for choosing a movie that featured dozens of zombies getting shot in the head.

When the movie was over, I called my wife, nine hours ahead in Italy.

"I should come home," she said.

"No, I'm okay," I said. "Come on, you're in Rome. What are you seeing today?"

"The Vatican."

"You can't leave now. You have to go and steal something. It will be revenge for every Indian. Or maybe you can plant an eagle feather and claim that you just discovered Catholicism."

"I'm worried."

"Yeah, Catholicism has always worried me."

"Stop being funny. I should see if I can get Mom and me on a flight tonight."

"No, no, listen, your mom is old. This might be her last adventure. It might be your last adventure with her. Stay there. Say Hi to the Pope for me. Tell him I like his shoes."

That night, my sons climbed into bed with me. We all slept curled around one another like sled dogs in a snowstorm. I woke, hour by hour, and touched my head and neck to check if they had changed shape—to feel if antennae were growing. Some insects "hear" with their antennae. Maybe that's what was happening to me.

9. Valediction

My father, a part-time blue collar construction worker, died in March 2003, from full-time alcoholism. On his deathbed he asked me to "Turn down that light, please."

"Which light?" I asked.

"The light on the ceiling."

"Dad, there's no light."

"It burns my skin, son. It's too bright. It hurts my eyes."

"Dad, I promise you there's no light."

"Don't lie to me, son, it's God passing judgment on Earth."

"Dad, you've been an atheist since '79. Come on, you're just remembering your birth. On your last day, you're going back to your first."

"No, son, it's God telling me I'm doomed. He's using the brightest lights in the universe to show me the way to my flame-filled tomb."

"No, Dad, those lights were in your delivery room."

"If that's true, son, then turn down my mother's womb."

We buried my father in the tiny Catholic cemetery on our reservation. Since I am named after him, I had to stare at a tombstone with my name on it.

10. Battle Fatigue

Two months after my father's death, I began research on a book about our family's history with war. I had a cousin who had served as a cook in the first Iraq war in 1991; I had another cousin who served in the Vietnam War in 1964–65, also as a cook; and my father's father, Adolph, served in WWII and was killed in action on Okinawa Island, on April 5, 1946.

During my research, I interviewed thirteen men who'd served with my cousin in Vietnam but could find only one surviving man who'd served with my grandfather. This is a partial transcript of that taped interview, recorded with a microphone and an iPod on January 14, 2008:

Me: Ah, yes, hello, I'm here in Livonia, Michigan, to interview—well, perhaps you should introduce yourself, please?

Leonard Elmore: What?

Me: Um, oh, I'm sorry, I was asking if you could perhaps introduce yourself.

LE: You're going to have to speak up. I think my hearing aid
is going low on power or something.

Me: That is a fancy thing in your ear.

LE: Yeah, let me mess with it a bit. I got a remote control for it. I can listen to the TV, the stereo, and the telephone with this thing. It's fancy. It's one of them blue tooth hearing aids. My grandson bought it for me. Wait, okay, there we go. I can hear now. So what were you asking?

Me: I was hoping you could introduce yourself into my recorder here.

LE: Sure, my name is Leonard Elmore.

Me: How old are you?

LE: I'm eighty-five-and-a-half years old (laughter). My great-grandkids are always saying they're seven-and-a-half or nine-and-a-half or whatever. It just cracks me up to say the same thing at my age.

Me: So, that's funny, um, but I'm here to ask you some questions about my grandfather—

LE: Adolph. It's hard to forget a name like that. An Indian named Adolph and there was that Nazi bastard named Adolph. Your grandfather caught plenty of grief over that. But we mostly called him "Chief," did you know that?

Me: I could have guessed.

LE: Yeah, nowadays, I suppose it isn't a good thing to call an Indian "Chief," but back then it was what we did. I served with a few Indians. They didn't segregate them Indians, you know, not like the black boys. I know you aren't supposed to call them boys anymore, but they were boys. All of us were boys, I guess. But the thing is, those Indian boys lived and slept and ate with us white boys. They were right there with us. But anyway, we called all them Indians "Chief." I bet you've been called "Chief" a few times yourself.

Me: Just once.

LE: Were you all right with it?

Me: I threw a basketball in the guy's face.

LE: (laughter)

Me: We live in different times.

LE: Yes, we do. Yes, we do.

Me: So perhaps you could, uh, tell me something about my grandfather.

LE: I can tell you how he died.

Me: Really?

LE: Yeah, it was on Okinawa, and we hit the beach and, well, it's hard to talk about it—it was the worst thing—it was Hell—no, that's not even a good way to describe it. I'm not a writer like you—I'm not a poet—so I don't have the words—but just think of it this way—that beach, that island—was filled with sons and fathers—men who loved and were loved—American and Japanese and Okinawan—and all of us were dying—were being killed by other sons and fathers who also loved and were loved.

Me: That sounds like poetry—tragic poetry—to me.

LE: Well, anyway, it was like that. Fire everywhere. And two of our boys—Jonesy and O'Neal—went down—were wounded in the open on the sand. And your grandfather—who was just this little man—barely five feet tall and maybe one hundred and thirty pounds—he just ran out there and picked up those two guys one on each shoulder—and carried them to cover. Hey, are you okay, son?

Me: Yes, I'm sorry. But, well, the thing is, I knew my grandfather was a war hero—he won twelve medals—but I could never find out what he did to win the medals.

LE: I didn't know about any medals. I just know what I saw. Your grandfather saved those two boys, but he got shot in the back doing it. And he laid there in the sand—I was lying right beside him and he died.

Me: Did he say anything before he died?

LE: Hold on. I need to—

Me: Are you okay?

LE: It's just—I can't—

Me: I'm sorry. Is there something wrong?

LE: No, it's just—with your book and everything—I know you want something big here. I know you want something big from your grandfather. I knew you hoped he'd said something huge and poetic, like maybe something you could have written, and, honestly, I was thinking about lying to you. I was thinking about making up something as beautiful as I could. Something about love and forgiveness and courage and all that. But I couldn't think of anything good enough. And I didn't want to lie to you. So I have to be honest and say that your grandfather didn't say anything. He just died there in the sand. In silence.

11. Orphans

I was worried that I had a brain tumor. Or that my hydrocephalus had returned. I was scared that I was going to die and orphan my sons. But, no, their mother was coming home from Italy. No matter what happened to me, their mother would rescue them.

"I'll be home in sixteen hours," my wife said over the phone.

"I'll be here," I said. "I'm just waiting on news from my doctor."

12. Coffee Shop News

While I waited, I asked my brother-in-law to watch the boys again because I didn't want to get bad news with them in the room.

Alone and haunted, I wandered the mall, tried on new clothes, and waited for my cell phone to ring.

Two hours later, I was uncomposed and wanted to murder everything, so I drove south to a coffee joint, a spotless place called Dirty Joe's.

Yes, I was silly enough to think that I'd be calmer with a caffeinated drink.

As I sat outside on a wooden chair and sipped my coffee, I cursed the vague, rumbling, ringing noise in my ear. And yet, when my cell phone rang, I held it to my deaf ear.

"Hello, hello," I said and wondered if it was a prank call, then remembered and switched the phone to my left ear.

"Hello," my doctor said. "Are you there?"

"Yes," I said. "So, what's going on?"

"There are irregularities in your head."

"My head's always been wrong."

"It's good to have a sense of humor," my doctor said. "You have a small tumor that is called a meningioma. They grow in the meninges membranes that lie between your brain and your skull."

"Shit," I said. "I have cancer."

"Well," my doctor said. "These kinds of tumors are usually noncancerous. And they grow very slowly, so in six months or so, we'll do another MRI. Don't worry. You're going to be okay."

"What about my hearing?" I asked.

"We don't know what might be causing the hearing loss, but you should start a course of prednisone, the steroid, just to go with the odds. Your deafness might lessen if left alone, but we've had success with the steroids in bringing back hearing. There *are* side effects, like insomnia, weight gain, night sweats, and depression."

"Oh, boy," I said. "Those side effects might make up most of my personality already. Will the 'roids also make me quick to pass judgment? And I've always wished I had a dozen more skin tags and moles."

The doctor chuckled. "You're a funny man."

I wanted to throw my phone into a wall but I said good-bye instead and glared at the tumorless people and their pretty tumorless heads.

13. Meningioma

Mayoclinic.com defines "meningioma" as "a tumor that arises from the meninges—the membranes that surround your brain and spinal cord. The majority of meningioma cases are noncancerous (benign), though rarely a meningioma can be cancerous (malignant)."

Okay, that was a scary and yet strangely positive definition. No one ever wants to read the word "malignant" unless one is reading a Charles Dickens novel about an evil landlord, but "benign" and "majority" are two things that go great together.

From the University of Washington Medical School Web site I learned that meningioma tumors "are usually benign, slow growing and do not spread into normal brain tissue. Typically, a meningioma grows inward, causing pressure on the brain or spinal cord. It may grow outward toward the skull, causing it to thicken."

So, wait, what the fuck? A meningioma can cause pressure on the brain and spinal fluid? Oh, you mean, just like fucking hydrocephalus? Just like the water demon that once tried to crush my brain and kill me? Armed with this new information—with these new questions—I called my doctor.

"Hey, you're okay," he said. "We're going to closely monitor you. And your meningioma is very small."

"Okay, but I just read—"

"Did you go on the Internet?"

"Yes."

"Which sites?"

"Mayo Clinic and the University of Washington."

"Okay, so those are pretty good sites. Let me look at them."

I listened to my doctor type.

"Okay, those are accurate," he said.

"What do you mean by accurate?" I asked. "I mean, the whole pressure on the brain thing, that sounds like hydrocephalus."

"Well, there were some irregularities in your MRI that were the burr holes from your surgery and there seems to be some scarring and perhaps you had an old concussion, but other than that, it all looks fine."

"But what about me going deaf? Can't these tumors make you lose hearing?"

"Yes, but only if they're located near an auditory nerve. And your tumor is not."

"Can this tumor cause pressure on my brain?"

"It could, but yours is too small for that."

"So, I'm supposed to trust you on the tumor thing when you can't figure out the hearing thing?"

"The MRI revealed the meningioma, but that's just an image. There is no physical correlation between your deafness and the tumor. Do the twenty-day treatment of prednisone and the audiologist and I will examine your ear, and your hearing. Then, if there's no improvement, we'll figure out other ways of treating you."

"But you won't be treating the tumor?"

"Like I said, we'll scan you again in six to nine months—"

"You said six before."

"Okay, in six months we'll take another MRI, and if it has grown significantly—or has changed shape or location or anything dramatic—then we'll talk about treatment options. But if you look on the Internet, and I know you're going to spend a lot of time obsessing on this—as you should—I'll tell you what you'll find. About 5 percent of the population has these things and they live their whole lives with these undetected meningiomas. And they can become quite large—without any side effects—and are only found at autopsies conducted for other causes of death. And even when these kinds of tumors become invasive or dangerous they are still rarely fatal. And your tumor, even if it grows fairly quickly, will not likely become an issue for many years, decades. So that's what I can tell you right now. How are you feeling?"

"Freaked and fucked."

I wanted to feel reassured, but I had a brain tumor. How does one feel any optimism about being diagnosed with a brain tumor? Even if that brain tumor is neither cancerous nor interested in crushing one's brain?

14. Drugstore Indian

In Bartell's Drugs, I gave the pharmacist my prescription for prednisone.

"Is this your first fill with us?" she asked.

"No," I said. "And it won't be the last."

I felt like an ass, but she looked bored.

"It'll take thirty minutes," she said, "more or less. We'll page you over the speakers."

I don't think I'd ever felt weaker, or more vulnerable, or more absurd. I was the weak antelope in the herd—yeah, the mangy fucker with the big limp and a sign that read, "Eat me! I'm a gimp!"

So, for thirty minutes, I walked through the store and found myself shoving more and more useful shit into my shopping basket, as if I were filling my casket with the things I'd need in the afterlife. I grabbed toothpaste, a Swiss Army knife, moisturizer, mouthwash, non-stick Band-Aids, antacid, protein bars, and extra razor blades. I grabbed pen and paper. And I also grabbed an ice scraper and sunscreen. Who can predict what weather awaits us in Heaven?

This random shopping made me feel better for a few minutes but then I stopped and walked to the toy aisle. My boys needed gifts: Lego cars or something, for a lift, a shot of capitalistic joy. But the selection of proper toys is art and science. I have been wrong as often as right and heard the sad song of a disappointed son.

Shit, if I died, I knew my sons would survive, even thrive, because of their graceful mother.

I thought of my father's life: he was just six when his father was killed in World War II. Then his mother, ill with tuberculosis, died a few months later. Six years old, my father was cratered. In most ways, he never stopped being six. There was no religion, no magic tricks, and no song or dance that helped my father.

Jesus, I needed a drink of water, so I found the fountain and drank and drank until the pharmacist called my name.

"Have you taken these before?" she asked.

"No," I said, "but they're going to kick my ass, aren't they?"

That made the pharmacist smile, so I felt sadly and briefly worthwhile. But another customer, some nosy hag, said, "You've got a lot of sleepless nights ahead of you."

I was shocked. I stammered, glared at her, and said, "Miss, how is this any of your business? Please, just fuck all the way off, okay?"

She had no idea what to say, so she just turned and walked away and I pulled out my credit card and paid far too much for my goddamn steroids, and forgot to bring the toys home to my boys.

15. Exit Interview for My Father

- True or False?: when a reservation-raised Native American dies of alcoholism it should be considered death by natural causes.
- Do you understand the term *wanderlust*, and if you do, can you please tell us, in twenty-five words or less, what place made you wanderlust the most?
- Did you, when drunk, ever get behind the tattered wheel of a '76 Ford three-speed van and somehow drive your family one thousand miles on an empty tank of gas?
- Is it true that the only literary term that has any real meaning in the Native American world is *road movie*?
- During the last road movie you saw, how many times did the characters ask, "Are we there yet?" How many times, during any of your road trips, did your children ask, "Are we there yet?"
- In twenty-five words or less, please define *there*.
- Sir, in your thirty-nine years as a parent, you broke your children's hearts, collectively and individually, 612 times and you did this without ever striking any human being in anger. Does this absence of physical violence make you a better man than you might otherwise have been?
- Without using the words *man* or *good*, can you please define what it means to be a good man?
- Do you think you will see angels before you die? Do you think angels will come to escort you to Heaven? As the angels are carrying you to Heaven, how many times will you ask, "Are we there yet?"
- Your son distinctly remembers stopping once or twice a month at that grocery store in Freeman, Washington, where you would buy him a red-white-and-blue rocket popsicle and purchase for yourself a pickled pig foot. Your son distinctly remembers the feet still had their toenails and little tufts of pig

fur. Could this be true? Did you actually eat such horrendous food?

- Your son has often made the joke that you were the only Indian of your generation who went to Catholic school on purpose. This is, of course, a tasteless joke that makes light of the forced incarceration and subsequent physical, spiritual, cultural, and sexual abuse of tens of thousands of Native American children in Catholic and Protestant boarding schools. In consideration of your son's questionable judgment in telling jokes, do you think there should be any moral limits placed on comedy?

- Your oldest son and your two daughters, all over thirty-six years of age, still live in your house. Do you think this is a lovely expression of tribal culture? Or is it a symptom of extreme familial codependence? Or is it both things at the same time?

- F. Scott Fitzgerald wrote that the sign of a superior mind "is the ability to hold two opposing ideas at the same time." Do you believe this is true? And is it also true that you once said, "The only time white people tell the truth is when they keep their mouths shut"?

- A poet once wrote, "Pain is never added to pain. It multiplies." Can you tell us, in twenty-five words or less, exactly how much we all hate mathematical blackmail?

- Your son, in defining you, wrote this poem to explain one of the most significant nights in his life:

Mutually Assured Destruction

> When I was nine, my father sliced his knee
> With a chain saw. But he let himself bleed
> And finished cutting down one more tree
> Before his boss drove him to EMERGENCY.
>
> Late that night, stoned on morphine and beer,
> My father needed my help to steer
> His pickup into the woods. "Watch for deer,"
> My father said. "Those things just appear
>
> Like magic." It was an Indian summer
> And we drove through warm rain and thunder
> Until we found that chain saw, lying under
> The fallen pine. Then I watched, with wonder,

As my father, shotgun-rich and impulse-poor,
Blasted that chain saw dead. "What was that for?"
I asked. "Son," my father said, "here's the score.
Once a thing tastes blood, it will come for more."

- Well, first of all, as you know, you did cut your knee with a chain saw, but in direct contradiction to your son's poem:

    A) You immediately went to the emergency room after injuring yourself.

    B) Your boss called your wife, who drove you to the emergency room.

    C) You were given morphine but even you were not alcoholically stupid enough to drink alcohol while on serious narcotics.

    D) You and your son did not get into the pickup that night.

    E) And even if you had driven the pickup, you were not injured seriously enough to need your son's help with the pedals and/or steering wheel.

    F) You never in your life used the word *appear* and certainly never used the phrase *like magic*.

    G) You also agree that Indian summer is a fairly questionable seasonal reference for an Indian poet to use.

    H) What the fuck is "warm rain and thunder"? Well, everybody knows what warm rain is, but what the fuck is warm thunder?

    I) You never went looking for that chain saw because it belonged to the Spokane tribe of Indians and what kind of freak would want to reclaim the chain saw that had just cut the shit out of his knee?

    J) You also agree that the entire third stanza of this poem sounds like a Bruce Springsteen song and not necessarily one of the great ones.

    K) And yet, "shotgun-rich and impulse-poor" is one of the greatest descriptions your son has ever written and probably redeems the entire poem.

    L) You never owned a shotgun. You did own a few rifles during your lifetime, but did not own even so much as a pellet gun during the last thirty years of your life.

    M) You never said, in any context, "Once a thing tastes your blood, it will come for more."

N) But you, as you read it, know that it is absolutely true and does indeed sound suspiciously like your entire life philosophy.

O) Other summations of your life philosophy include: "I'll be there before the next teardrop falls."

P) And: "If God really loved Indians, he would have made us white people."

Q) And: "Oscar Robertson should be the man on the NBA logo. They only put Jerry West on there because he's a white guy."

R) And: "A peanut butter sandwich with onions. Damn, that's the way to go."

S) And: "Why eat a pomegranate when you can eat a plain old apple. Or peach. Or orange. When it comes to fruit and vegetables, only eat the stuff you know how to grow."

T) And: "If you really want a woman to love you, then you have to dance. And if you don't want to dance, then you're going to have to work extra hard to make a woman love you forever, and you will always run the risk that she will leave you at any second for a man who knows how to tango."

U) And: "I really miss those cafeterias they used to have in Kmart. I don't know why they stopped having those. If there is a Heaven then I firmly believe it's a Kmart cafeteria."

V) And: "A father always knows what his sons are doing. For instance, boys, I knew you were sneaking that *Hustler* magazine out of my bedroom. You remember that one? Where actors who looked like Captain Kirk and Lieutenant Uhura were screwing on the bridge of the *Enterprise*. Yeah, that one. I know you kept borrowing it. I let you borrow it. Remember this: men and pornography are like plants and sunshine. To me, porn is photosynthesis."

W) And: "Your mother is a better man than me. Mothers are almost always better men than men are."

16. Reunion

After she returned from Italy, my wife climbed into bed with me. I felt like I had not slept comfortably in years.

I said, "There was a rumor that I'd grown a tumor but I killed it with humor."

"How long have you been waiting to tell me that one?" she asked.

"Oh, probably since the first time some doctor put his fingers in my brain."

We made love. We fell asleep. But I, agitated by the steroids, woke at two, three, four, and five a.m. The bed was killing my back so I lay flat on the floor. I wasn't going to die anytime soon, at least not because of my little friend, Mr. Tumor, but that didn't make me feel any more comfortable or comforted. I felt distant from the world—from my wife and sons, from my mother and siblings—from all of my friends. I felt closer to those who've always had fingers in their brains.

And I didn't feel any closer to the world six months later when another MRI revealed that my meningioma had not grown in size or changed its shape.

"You're looking good," my doctor said. "How's your hearing?"

"I think I've got about 90 percent of it back."

"Well, then, the steroids worked. Good."

And I didn't feel any more intimate with God nine months later when one more MRI made my doctor hypothesize that my meningioma might only be more scar tissue from the hydrocephalus.

"Frankly," my doctor said, "your brain is beautiful."

"Thank you," I said, though it was the oddest compliment I'd ever received.

I wanted to call up my father and tell him that a white man thought my brain was beautiful. But I couldn't tell him anything. He was dead. I told my wife and sons that I was okay. I told my mother and siblings. I told my friends. But none of them laughed as hard about my beautiful brain as I knew my father would have. I miss him, the drunk bastard. I would always feel closest to the man who had most disappointed me.

Acknowledgments

Alexie, Sherman. "War Dances," from *War Dances*. Copyright © 2009 by Sherman Alexie. Used by permission of Grove/Atlantic, Inc. Any third party use of this material, outside of this publication, is prohibited.

Bruchac III, Joseph. "Turtle Meat," from *Earth Power Coming: Short Fiction in Native American Literature,* Navajo Community College Press, Tsaile, Arizona. 1983. Copyright © 1983 by Joseph Bruchac III. Reprinted by permission of the author.

Forbes, Jack D. "Only Approved Indians Can Play Made in USA," from *Only Approved Indians: Stories*. University of Oklahoma Press, 1995. Reprinted by permission of University of Oklahoma Press.

Funaro, Eli. "The Dog Pit," from *Both Sides: New Work from the Institute of American Indian Arts*, 1993–1994. Santa Fe: The Institute of American Indian Arts. 1994. Copyright © by Eli Funaro. Reprinted by permission of the author.

Green, Rayna. "High Cotton," from *That's What She Said: Contemporary Poetry and Fiction by Native American Women*. Edited by Rayna Green. Indiana University Press. 1984. Reprinted by permission of Indiana University Press.

Johnson, Pauline. "A Red Girl's Reasoning," from the *Dominion Illustrated* (Canada). February 1893.

King, Thomas. "Borders," from *One Good Story, That One*. (HarperCollins, 1993; New Edition, 1999). Copyright © 1993 Dead Dog Café Productions, Inc. Used by permission of the author.

McNickle, Darcy. "Train Time," from *Indians at Work 3*. Washington, D.C.: Bureau of Indian Affairs. March 15, 1936.

Niatum, Duane. "Crow's Sun," from *Talking Leaves: Contemporary Native American Short Stories*. Edited by Craig Lesley. New York: Dell Publishing. 1991. Reprinted by permission of the author.

Oskison, John M. "The Singing Bird," from *Sunset Magazine*. March 1925.

Piatote, Beth: "Beading Lesson," from *Reckonings: Contemporary Short Fiction by Native American Women*. Hertha D. Sweet Wong, Lauren Stuart Muller, Jana Sequoya Magdaleno, editors. New York: Oxford University Press. 2008. Copyright © by Beth Piatote. Reprinted by permission of the author.

Silko, Leslie Marmon. "The Man to Send Rainclouds," from *Storyteller* by Leslie Marmon Silko. Copyright © 1981, 2012 by Leslie Marmon Silko. Used by permission of Viking Penguin, a division of Penguin Group (USA) LLC, and The Wylie Agency (UK) Limited.

TallMountain, Mary. "Snatched Away," from *Talking Leaves: Contemporary Native American Short Stories*. Edited by Craig Lesley. New York: Dell Publishing. 1991. Copyright © 1994 by the TallMountain Estate. All rights reserved. Reprinted by permission of the TallMountain Estate.

Zitkala-Sa: "The Soft-Hearted Sioux," from *Harper's Monthly* 102. (March 1901).